W9-BVU-188

THE SAINT AND
THE TEMPLAR TREASURE

It was, to say the least, an intriguing situation. A noble family plagued by a curse that was being helped to work by a couple of small-time crooks. A proud and beautiful young woman too well aware of her station to show her emotions openly, but most certainly a very frightened female. A magnificent house that had about it a feeling of foreboding as if even the walls were waiting for something to happen . . . Chance had brought the Saint to the Château Ingare, in Provence. But when his visit entangled him in a bitter struggle for the mysterious treasure of the Knights Templar, he couldn't help feeling that Fate had a hand in it too.

Leslie Charteris'
THE SAINT AND THE TEMPLAR TREASURE

Original outline by
Donne Avenell
Developed by
Graham Weaver

A Lythway Book

CHIVERS PRESS
BATH

First published in Great Britain 1978
by
Coronet Books
This Large Print edition published by
Chivers Press
by arrangement with
Hodder and Stoughton Limited
and in the U.S.A. and Canada with
Doubleday & Company, Inc
1986

ISBN 0 7451 0387 1

British Library Cataloguing in Publication Data

Avenell, Donne
   Leslie Charteris' the Saint and the Templar
treasure.—(A Lythway book)
I. Title   II. Weaver, Graham, *1949*—
III. Charteris, Leslie
823'.914[F]   PR6061.I43

ISBN 0–7451–0387–1

CONTENTS

CHAPTER ONE

HOW SIMON TEMPLAR DISCOVERED A WINE, AND FOUND HIMSELF STUCK WITH IT

Serious bibbers of wine tend to come in two classes. Discounting those who differentiate between bottles only by the colour of the contents, there are those who know a little and talk a lot, and those who know a lot and talk little. Simon Templar was numbered among the latter.

The mystique that so often surrounds the appreciation of wine left him cold. He was indifferent to which side of the hill the grape had flourished on. Knowledge of the shoe size of the head grape-treader left him unmoved. He found the family antecedents of the vigneron of yawning interest. All he was really concerned about was that the quality should be outstanding, without fretting too much over the technical trivia through which the quality had been achieved.

Fine wines, like good food, beautiful women, elegant clothes, and fast cars, were facets of a life-style to which he had happily become accustomed. He could survive without such

1

trappings, but he saw no reason to do so if he could afford them. They helped to make life exciting and that was a spice that he demanded.

The liquid which he was transferring from bottle to glass, that afternoon in one of the infant years of what had been optimistically hailed as the new era of World Peace at Last when it was signed in 1945, certainly answered that criterion. The *sommelier*, who was also the *maître d'hotel* and the *patron*, had suggested and he had accepted a local product which he had never heard of before, and for him it was now a memorable discovery. He sipped again the deep red, almost purple, wine and savoured the strong fruity bouquet characteristic of the slopes of the Rhône. It was a taste that he would remember for the rest of his life; but at that moment he was blissfully unaware of what that chance sampling was destined eventually to involve him in and make itself totally unforgettable.

The wine was not the first new experience of the day. After leaving Avignon he had turned off the main road to wander through the back lanes of the countryside in search of a restaurant which had been recommended to him by a friend of impeccable discrimination, one of those epicurean hideaways to be found dotted around France whose whereabouts are the jealously guarded secret of an inner circle of gourmets, until somebody leaks it to the *Guide*

2

Michelin and the clientele and the prices take off on their inevitable escalade.

The building which he had finally found had previously been a watermill and was set back from the road beside a narrow stream that gurgled under the now stationary waterwheel on its way down the valley towards the winding ribbon of the Rhône. The new owners had possessed the sense to keep the transformation simple. The dining area was a long high-ceilinged room that looked as if it had once served as a storehouse. The roof beams had been left rough and unstained, a few undemanding prints had been hung against the stone walls, and some rugs scattered across the flagged floor. The walls had been broken through to provide additional windows that allowed broad bands of sunlight to enter, while strategically placed electric fans kept the heat of the early autumn sun at bay.

In such a setting it was possible to concentrate on the important business of eating and drinking, unlike so many pretentious restaurants where the purpose of the décor is to intimidate criticisms of the cuisine and the tariff being paid for the privilege of eating it. The food had in fact justified everything that his discerning friend had claimed for it: the *queues d'écrevisses aux morilles* had been a delightfully delicate surprise, and the *gigot à la ficelle*, boldly seasoned with herbs and garlic and roasted

3

before an open wood fire, was worthy of an oldfashioned highwayman's appetite.

Except for a few accidental holidaymakers who had had the good fortune to stumble on the restaurant by chance, his fellow customers had a general air of more sophisticated self-indulgence than one would have expected to find in such a rural setting. At the next table a large florid man whose buttons showed the strain of many years of dedicated gluttony was chomping through a double helping of *alouettes sur canapé*. Simon found the spectacle of such a big man devouring so many small birds both comical and sad, and turned his attention to the others in the room. Most of them, he guessed, must have made an excursion from one of the more important cities of Provence, if not from even farther afield, lured by the reports that circulated through the gastronomic grapevine.

Occasionally the other clients would glance across in their turn to where he sat, stare for a moment, and then return to their plates. There was something familiar about his face. Something slightly unsettling about the lean tanned features and the clear blue eyes with their light of mocking challenge. Something intangibly dangerous in the easy grace with which he sat alone in a corner, which might have reminded the more imaginative among them of a panther watching its prey at play before pouncing.

4

Simon Templar was resigned to arousing such interest. His days of anonymity were already somewhat past. His picture was to be found in the files of every major newspaper from New York to New Delhi and of every police department from Scotland Yard to Sydney— filed not under T for Templar, but S for Saint.

The same imaginative diner who sensed the predator behind his untroubled relaxation, even without identifying him, would probably have speculated on the reason for his presence; and the more fanciful assumptions would, as usual, have found most favour. But they would have been wrong, for the Saint's sole motive was to enjoy the best of solid and liquid calories that would fuel the rest of his projected drive to St Tropez.

The Saint had been to Valencia with no more nefarious intent than to assess for himself the talent of the latest *fenomenón* of the bullring, a rising young matador whom he had been reading about; but, as he found so much pleasure in business that he felt no need to separate the two, it had proved a profitable vacation. A certain promoter of dubious real estate developments on the Costa Blanca, secure in the knowledge that the long arm of the British law could not touch him there, but who had forgotten that outlaws have an even lengthier reach, had costly reason to regret having been brought by chance to his notice. On the other

5

hand, there had been Margarita, who would always have a happy memory—but that is another story.

Simon had been driving back at a leisurely pace, allowing time to take in the sights along the way like any tourist. He had spent a day and a night in Avignon, where he had walked the battlements of the medieval walls, filed with other sightseers through the Cathedral of Notre-Dame-des-Doms and the palace of the Popes, and tried to theorise about what kind of dancing could have caused the collapse of the famous bridge. So much history had proved rather suffocating, and the uncluttered lanes of the countryside and the finding of the restaurant to which they had led him had been particularly welcome.

But now his watch told him it was time to be moving again, and he drained his glass with genuine regret. He declined coffee and cognac so that he could retain the lingering after taste of the wine, and asked for his bill.

While he waited he picked up the bottle and studied the label again. It was simple to the point of plainness. Just the name of the vineyard—Château Ingare—above the date of the vintage. The only decoration was a discreet family crest consisting of an open shield with a crusader's helmet in one half and an upright sword in the other. Since the name was completely new to him—a surprising fact in

6

view of the quality of the wine and his own empirical knowledge of the product of the region—it could only have been a very limited but very special family affair, generating only enough for a select and exclusive distribution.

The Saint rose and paid the bill, leaving a generous tip, thanked and congratulated the *patron*, and sauntered out into the early afternoon sunshine. After the pleasant temperature of the restaurant the fierce dry heat of the valley seemed even more intense than it had done during the drive from Avignon that morning. He walked slowly to where the Hirondel was parked. The flamboyant cream and red roadster was surrounded by the sedate black sedans of the townsmen. A car like the Hirondel in such company looked like a Derby winner stabled in a donkey shed.

He eased in behind the wheel, being careful to touch as little of the searing-hot coachwork as possible. From the rear seat he retrieved a battered grey fedora that would have made Mr Lock pale, and snapped the brim down to shade his eyes from the sun's glare. The motor turned at the first touch and the purr of the perfectly tuned engine changed to a muted roar as he swung the big car around and headed towards the road.

The entrance to the parking space was partly hidden from the lane by a clump of trees, and half the bonnet of the Hirondel had passed them before the strident blare of a klaxon and a screech of tyres made him stamp on the brake. A small blue Renault convertible swerved violently across his front fender before the driver brought it back under control and, with an angry glare at the Saint, lurched on and disappeared at speed around the next bend.

The Saint smiled. Such a driver could, he decided, glare angrily at him anytime, preferably when she was not in so great a hurry and at even closer quarters. Long black hair riding the slipstream, a small oval face that might almost have been plain had it not been made beautiful by a pair of dark flashing eyes, plus the upper contours of a figure that promised much for those areas of anatomy hidden by the car's own bodywork.

He carried the image with him as he threaded the Hirondel gently through the spider's web of meandering lanes which he hoped would eventually bring him back on to some adequately signposted highway on which he could set a course in the general direction of Aix-en-Provence. He was in no hurry, and the tranquillising effect of his lunch made him decide against pursuing the Renault and telling its owner his thoughts about women drivers. Which, he later reflected, was just as well, for it would have closed the story before it opened.

The road he was on ended in a T-junction. A signpost stated that Avignon was now somewhere to his right but gave no indication of what lay to the left. Being reasonably sure that at least he should not head back towards Avignon, even though the other way might be leading north, he gambled and swung the wheel to port. It was a decision that brought him one step closer to the start of the adventure.

2

The vine is an amazingly stubborn vegetable that seems to flourish best in the worst conditions. In Portugal's High Douro they are stuck into holes drilled in solid rock, while beside the Mosel they prosper on precipitous slopes of almost pure slate. Beside the road along which the Saint finally found himself driving, the ground seemed capable of producing only stones, but it was patterned with neat rows of low-growing vines. In the distance, a low line of hills had been terraced to provide a root-hold for still more plants, giving the appearance of a huge overgrown staircase. The lower slopes and terraces were littered with bleached boulders from fist to head size that absorbed the sun's rays during the day and slowly released their stored heat through the night, providing the plants with natural central heating.

It was late September, and the vines were bending under the weight of their dark purple fruit. To the layman's eye they all looked the same, but up to fourteen varieties might be blended to create such a beverage as the Saint had enjoyed at lunch. The harvest would begin any day, and the now deserted landscape would be alive with workers gathering the grapes and carting it back to the presses for the start of the time-honoured process of making the wine.

Simon was musing idly on the years it could take to produce a great wine compared to the minutes it takes to drink one, when he spotted the two hikers. Even from a distance they seemed an oddly mismatched pair. One was tall and blond with broad shoulders that made light of the heavy haversack he carried. He wore a white short-sleeved shirt, faded khaki shorts and tough walking boots, and strode steadily along at an even pace. A step behind and struggling to keep up limped his companion. He was smaller and fatter and his clothes seemed more suitable for city shopping than for hiking. His back was bowed beneath a small pack and a blue jacket slung over one shoulder that matched the serge of his tight-fitting trousers and complemented his equally tight-fitting shoes. As he heard the Hirondel approaching he turned, and the pleading look on his face was more eloquent than his raised thumb.

The Saint normally had little sympathy for hitch-hikers, holding that the hyphenation was itself a contradiction in terms, and feeling no obligation to provide free transport for those who were too lazy to walk or too imprudent to provide themselves with even a bicycle. But that afternoon caught him in a relaxed and mellow mood.

He brought the Hirondel to a gliding halt, and said in fluent French: 'You seem ready to melt. Where are you going?'

Simon Templar was at ease in all the major languages of Europe and could make himself understood in most of the remainder. He spoke French as well as any native of that country and possibly better than many. Unlike so many English speakers he did not suffer from the arrogance which expects that everyone else should know the language which once ruled an empire and believes that if they don't the way to make them understand it is to shout.

The blond youth—both of them looked to be in their late teens or earliest twenties—answered: 'To Carpentras, then towards Beaumes-de-Venise.'

'And where the devil would that be?' Simon enquired cautiously.

'Not very far. I can show you the way.'

The Saint shrugged. Having made the stop, he might as well take the consequences.

'Well, that may be useful. Hop in.'

They heaved their packs into the narrow back seat where the smaller hitch-hiker also wedged himself, while his blond companion settled more comfortably in the front. Simon released the handbrake and as the car moved forward asked: 'Where are you from?'

'The University of Grenoble. We are students. My name is Pascal, and he is Jules.'

In his driving mirror the saint had a picture of Jules dabbing at his sweating face with a handkerchief and flapping the open front of his shirt to allow the breeze to circulate.

'Your friend doesn't seem in training for a route march,' he observed drily.

Pascal smiled.

'He is from Paris,' he explained in a condescending tone. 'He thinks a stroll in the Bois de Boulogne is exhausting.'

'And you're a country boy, is that it?'

'I was born at Châteauneuf and my family lived here until four years ago when we moved to Lyons. Since then I have come back every year to help with the harvest and to see my old friends. Jules thought he would come along this year to earn some money.'

'From what I know of work in the vineyards he is likely to lose more kilos than he gains francs,' said the Saint.

Pascal laughed, but the object of their conversation either had not heard or was too tired to object.

They drove in silence for a few minutes before Simon asked: 'Where exactly will you be working?'

'At Château Ingare. It is only a small vineyard

and they do not pay as well as some of the larger ones, but all my friends will be there.'

The name had produced a creeping sensation across the Saint's scalp that he could not explain, as if some sixth sense was trying to warn him. But of what? There was nothing really surprising in the fact that he should drink a bottle of local wine and then meet two people on their way to the vineyard that produced it. Just a minor coincidence of course, but he could never accept coincidences entirely at their face value, just as years of living on a knife's edge had taught him never to dismiss the instincts that such an existence had developed.

'Tell me about Château Ingare, Pascal,' he said thoughtfully, and the youth seemed happy to oblige.

'As I said, it is one of the smaller vineyards, but also one of the oldest. It has been in the Florian family for generations—in fact since the fourteenth century. The château itself is one of the most beautiful in the region. It was originally a castle and stands on a hill above the vineyards. From it you can see to the horizon.

'The family settled here around the time the Popes first built their summer palace at Châteauneuf. All this area around Avignon belonged not to France but to the Papacy, right up until the Revolution. It was they who planted some of the first vines.'

'Is that why they call Châteauneuf the Pope of

13

wines?' Simon suggested.

'Perhaps; though it wasn't the wine of Popes, apparently. It is said they preferred Burgundy.'

'I tried a bottle of Château Ingare for the first time today.' The Saint was impelled to keep the conversation going in that direction. 'It was excellent. Why haven't I heard about it before?'

'Yes, it is very good,' Pascal agreed enthusiastically. 'But unfortunately it is rarely sold outside this area because only a small quantity is produced, and the family do not have the hectares to extend their market.'

'Noble but poor?' Simon prompted. 'Do you know the family?'

Pascal wagged his head noncommittally.

'I am sure there is a lot to tell, but I do not know very much of it except that the war almost bankrupted the estate. Monsieur Yves, he is the head of the family, vowed that he would never make wine for the Germans, so every year the grapes were picked and pressed, and every year something happened. One year all the bottles were mysteriously broken, another year the wine was contaminated, and so it went on. Even when the Germans took over the château and billeted their officers there the accidents continued.'

'That must have been an expensive piece of resistance,' the Saint commented.

'Very expensive. But since the war ended there have been other troubles. There is a

legend locally that the Florian family is cursed,'
Pascal added hesitantly.

'Vineyard workers are traditionally as
superstitious as sailors,' said the Saint with a
smile. 'And who do they think cursed the
family—the Germans?'

Pascal laughed harshly and said: 'I think their
methods of punishment were more direct. But
the curse on the Florian family is supposed to be
much older. In fact, it goes back to the
Templiers.'

The name, dropped quite casually, sounded
in the Saint's ears like a tocsin.

Whereas a little earlier the recall of Château
Ingare had caused only an almost caressing
frisson at the roots of his hair, this new
association set off a whole jangling of psychic
alarm bells which no facile scepticism could
silence.

For the translation of *Templier* is 'Templar',
and *les Templiers* is the French word for what
English historians call the Knights Templar—
from whom, in the remote past, some ancestor
of Simon's must have taken his patronym.

'The legend is that the castle was built by the
Templars, and when they fled it is said they
cursed whoever should own it next.'

Although the Saint had always been aware of
the historic connotation of his unusual name, he
had never taken much interest in the snob sport
of ancestor-tracing, and in fact had not even

bothered to study the subject of the original Templars. He had a vague idea that they had protected pilgrims on their way to the Holy Land and had fought with distinction in the Crusades. He confessed as much to Pascal without revealing his own identity, and the young student seemed pleased to be given the chance to show off his own erudition.

He explained how they had banded together at the beginning of the eleventh century and had taken their title from the temple in Jerusalem, swearing to win back the city for the Christians and rebuild the temple. Their bravery in battle and support for the Christian cause had won them the extremely rare privilege of appointing their own bishops and being answerable only to the Pope himself.

'By the end of the thirteenth century there were more than twenty thousand Knights in Europe,' Pascal continued, 'and they were the single most powerful organisation on the continent. They owned vast areas of land, paid no taxes, and were often far wealthier than kings. They wore a surcoat with an eight-pointed cross on it which guaranteed them immunity wherever they went, and because they were so powerful they began to be feared.'

The Saint thought of his own emblem of a haloed matchstick figure and the near supernatural awe that it had once inspired among the ranks of the Ungodly, before it had become so famous as to be virtually unusable any more.

'Jealousy bred rumours,' Pascal went on. 'It was said that initiates had to spit on the Cross, that the Knights were often homosexuals and that many of them practised black magic. As the Crusades failed, they concentrated on increasing their wealth and power and became generally corrupt.'

'A sort of medieval Mafia,' Simon murmured approvingly.

'In a way, yes. Eventually, under pressure, the Pope outlawed them and they were persecuted throughout Europe. Very many were tortured and burned. In France they were completely wiped out.'

'Was that what happened to the Templars at Château Ingare?'

Pascal shook his head.

'No. They were besieged for many weeks by the King's army, but somehow most of them escaped just before the walls were breached. That is probably why there are so many legends about the place, for the Knights were never seen again and no one knows where the survivors went.'

At least one of them, the Saint figured, must have found his way to England. He decided that one day he would have to do some more research into his infamous ancestry.

A road sign told him that they were just

entering the town of Carpentras, and with a trace of reluctance he enquired: 'Which way do you go from here?'

'Château Ingare is to the north, but perhaps that is not your direction.'

Pascal turned and considered his friend, who appeared to have fallen into a light doze. He leaned over and prodded him sharply in the stomach, and the youth stirred and sat up. Pascal turned back to the Saint.

'It is only a few kilometres and I think Jules has had enough rest.'

A low moan of protest from Jules showed that he did not agree with his friend, but the Saint had already made his decision. At the next signposted intersection he spun the wheel to the left.

'Since I've come this far out of my way, a few more kilometres are not going to make much difference. And they might even let me buy a few bottles to take home with me.'

His tone was matter-of-fact but his eyes narrowed as he spoke. There was a strange, almost eerie, tingle of excitement beginning to bubble in the pit of his stomach, a tightening of nerves for which there was no logical explanation. He tried to shake off the feeling, but instead it grew stronger as the miles were covered.

Two coincidences involving the Château Ingare could be brushed off; but the third,

18

linking it with his own name, looked too much like the weaving of fate to be a fluke. Even in his moods of most determined realism, Simon Templar had an Achilles heel for the sense of destiny that had made his life so different from all other lives.

After a while, following Pascal's directions, he turned off the secondary D7 on to an even lesser road that wound up a range of rocky but still vine-clad foothills. As they came over one of the lower rises he saw the smoke. It was curling into the sky from beyond a copse of tall cypresses, halfway up the hillside about half a mile away.

'Looks like a fire,' he observed casually.

Pascal's reaction was more dramatic.

'*C'est la grange!*'

'Does it belong to the château?' Simon asked, and already seemed to know the answer before the lad replied.

'It is where everything is stored ready for the *récolte*. They would not light a fire there!'

Before the final word was spoken the Saint was on his way. In a synchronised flow of movements he flicked the gear lever into third and pressed the accelerator towards the floor as the clutch bit. The big car awoke like a jungle cat, roared and catapulted itself forward.

If he had had any lingering doubt, the last trace of it had vanished. He knew now that all his premonitions had been right, and that he was irretrievably caught again in the web of Kismet.

3

Like a bolt from a crossbow the Hirondel sped towards its target. The lane snaked into a chicane of S bends, and the two students grabbed desperately at the side of the car as the Saint threw it into the corners with one hand juggling the steering wheel as the other changed gear with a smooth confidence that would have done credit to any Grand Prix professional. But then, the Saint could have qualified as one of those himself if he had not chosen a more hazardous way of life.

Just around the second curve, a horse-drawn cart suddenly appeared in front of him, barely fifteen yards ahead and taking up almost two-thirds of the road. There was no time to stop and not enough room between the cart and the high sloping bank on the clearer side for the Hirondel to overtake.

A thin smile touched the Saint's lips as he kept his foot on the accelerator and turned the wheel to the left. For an instant it seemed certain that they must plough into either the bank or the cart or both, but he had judged the angle of the slope and his own speed to perfection.

The Hirondel mounted the bank and seemed to hang poised in the air for the space of a heartbeat before the left rear wheel gripped and he could reverse the steering to bring the car parallel to the road. He caught a blurred glimpse of the drayman's amazed expression, and then they were past and bumping back on to the solid tarmac of the lane in a shower of dust and small pebbles, safely in front of the equally startled horse.

'That's how the stunt men do it in the movies,' he informed his ashen-faced passengers as he negotiated the next bend without slackening speed.

Pascal said nothing but continued to clutch at the door, his knees braced to absorb the impact he felt must come at any second. In the rear-view mirror, Jules looked as if he was about to be sick.

The lane had climbed enough by then to give them a sight of several buildings rising picturesquely beyond the screen of cypress. The smoke was thicker now, with the original light grey spiral streaked with ominous black.

'The track to the barn is beyond those posts,' Pascal said breathlessly, pointing to a narrow opening ahead.

The Saint nodded and heeled the car around between the white-painted posts with an inch to spare on either wing.

The track ran diagonally across the sloping hillside to the copse where it was hidden by the trees before continuing towards the complex of

21

other buildings. The surface was sun-cracked mud thinly covered by gravel-sized fragments of crushed boulders. It had been designed for horses and tractors rather than low-slung sports cars, and their progress was accompanied by the rattle of stones flung against the chassis like hail against a window. At any moment he expected to hear a roar as the exhaust was ripped away, but their luck held and they reached the trees without apparent harm.

What had looked like a thick copse from a distance turned out to be simply a double row of cypress planted close together to act as a windbreak to the north of the vineyard, and also to provide some shade for the workers between their spells of labour. Beyond the trees was a long low-roofed barn, its walls made from the hillside rocks and looking capable of withstanding a broadside of twentyfive pounders. But the timbers of the roof were clearly more vulnerable. Already the far end was well alight, and the flames were licking greedily along the ridge and eaves. It could only be a matter of minutes before the whole roof would be ablaze.

A black Citroën was parked in front of the barn facing back down the track. Simon pulled the Hirondel to a protesting halt beside it. He vaulted out of the car and was sprinting towards the building even before the last piston had come to rest.

Two massive double doors comprised most of the end of the barn nearest to him, but he ignored them and ran towards the small service door that stood open halfway along the side.

As he approached two men ran out. The first was tall in a wide-lapelled pinstripe suit with shoulders padded almost to the width of the doorway he had just emerged from. The second was a head shorter but huskier and wore a black leather zipper jacket and baggy black corduroys. They looked so much like the classical double act of a Hollywood B picture that the Saint felt the laughter rising within him. But he paid them the compliment of lengthening his stride, well aware that even cliché crooks can carry guns.

At the sight of the Saint racing towards them the two men looked uncertainly at each other, their expressions showing that they had not anticipated any trouble. As Simon reached them the big man lashed out at the place where the Saint's head should have been. But the target was no longer there. The Saint ducked low, his left hand catching the man's wrist as his right arm flashed between his legs. The man yelled in pain as the Saint's arm jarred up into his crotch, and in the same fluid movement Simon rose out of his crouch and the man felt his feet lose contact with the ground as he was held in an excruciating parody of a fireman's lift, before the Saint stepped out from under him and left the force of gravity to help the unlucky arsonist return to earth.

The Saint looked enquiringly at his leather-clad sidekick, but the latter turned and scooted towards the Citroën. Out of the corner of his eye, Simon saw Pascal make a grab for him and shouted: 'Leave him. There's an extinguisher in my car, get it.'

He pointed to a standpipe at the corner of the barn.

'And you should know where to find a hose. Tell Jules!'

Without waiting to watch his orders carried out, he plunged into the barn.

The open door had created an updraught that had pushed the eddying billows of smoke back up into the roof, and the Saint was able to see the general layout and take stock of the situation. It was worse than he had feared.

The flames he had seen from the outside were nothing compared to those rapidly engulfing the triangles of beams supporting the roof. The far end of the barn where the fire had clearly been started was already an inferno, and an open loft stacked with wickerwork hoppers was beyond saving. Even as he watched he saw the plank floor sag and heard the timbers crack under the strain. Sparks from the beams had kindled half a dozen smaller fires among heaps of baskets by the walls, which in turn were igniting a line of wooden hand carts.

A truck was parked in the centre of the

24

building facing the double doors and he made his way towards it. The deeper he moved into the barn the denser the smoke became and by the time he reached the lorry his eyes were running with water. He knelt down and sucked the fresher air nearer the floor into his lungs while he considered his next move.

The barn had been stocked with everything needed for the coming harvest. The baskets and hoppers would be used to carry the grapes from the fields to where the truck would transport them back to the *chai* for pressing. He remembered Pascal's talk of the recent accidents that had plagued the vineyard and smiled grimly.

It was obvious that the building was doomed but he refused to admit total defeat so quickly.

'Whatever makes anyone want to be a fireman?' he asked himself as he wiped the water from his eyes with the sleeve of his jacket and stood up.

As he did so the floor of the loft finally gave way and crashed down in an explosion of sparks. Some of the burning spars fell across the open door, cutting off any attempt at retreat in that direction. The entire roof was alight now and the heat scorched his face as he ran to the cab of the truck.

The vehicle was of pre-war lineage, and he cursed as he realised that self-starters had been considered a luxury when it had first been put on the road. He pulled himself up into the cab and gave silent thanks when he saw that the key had at least been left in the ignition. He turned it and jumped out again. The smoke was becoming thicker every second and it was all he could do to see his way to the front of the radiator. Every breath was becoming a painful effort, and he knew that if the starting handle was not already in place there would be no time to search for it. But again the gods were with him, and he took hold of it and began to crank the engine.

At the first turn the engine coughed. At the second it spluttered briefly and died again. Sparks rained down on him and threatened to singe his hair and clothes. His chest felt as if he had swallowed vitriol, but he calmly swung the handle a third time, stubbornly refusing to be beaten. And the old engine, as if realising that this was its last chance, fired and kept running.

The Saint stumbled back into the cab. The beams above him were burning fiercely, and he knew that they could only last for a few minutes. There was no time to unbar the double doors, and he prayed fervently that the engine would not stall. He released the handbrake and gently engaged the gears. The run-up was only a few feet, and he opened the throttle wide as the truck moved forward.

He hit the double doors squarely in the centre. For one paralysing moment they seemed to hold before the metal bolts were ripped from their mountings and they flew open under the impact.

Simon kept the truck moving until the building was a safe distance behind him before he stopped. In the same instant the roof of the barn collapsed.

The Saint gulped down the clean air as he used his handkerchief to mop the sweat from his forehead. As he waited for the adrenalin to dissolve and his pulse rate to subside he looked in the driver's mirror and discovered the ravages to his appearance. Most areas of his face that were not powdered with ash were smeared with soot. His eyes were bloodshot, and the front of what ten minutes before had been a spotless white shirt was sodden and grimy.

'One day I should learn to mind my own business,' he told his reflection disgustedly, and turned to climb out of the cab.

He placed one hand on the open window and quickly drew it away as a searing twinge shot up his arm. He looked at the blackened burn on his palm in amazement. A smouldering ember must have fallen from the roof and lodged on the sill, but he had been so busy with more urgent problems that he had not even noticed it. Now, as the excitement wore off, the penalty of his preoccupation was more exasperating than painful. He twisted his handkerchief angrily over the injury and swung himself down to the ground.

The Citroën and the arsonists had disappeared. Pascal and Jules were running towards him.

'Are you all right?' they shouted.

'As you see,' Simon replied.

'There was nothing we could do,' panted Jules. 'No buckets, no hose, nothing.'

'I emptied your extinguisher, but it was not enough,' Pascal said. 'When the door was blocked I thought you would never come out.' He noticed the Saint's handkerchief bandage. 'Are you sure you are not hurt?'

'I'll mend.'

'They got away,' said Jules apologetically.

'You told us to leave them,' Pascal put in quickly.

'But I got the number of their car,' said Jules proudly, and the Saint clapped him on the shoulder.

'Well done. That's something, anyway.'

He was prepared to lay ten to one that the car had been stolen, but it would have been mean to have disparaged the lad's achievement.

While they had been talking he had been watching a battered jeep coming down the drive from the château. It stopped by the barn and its crew of four jumped out. Two of them were obviously outdoor workers on the estate, and leading them was a much older man and a young girl, who had been driving. Even in that situation, the French ritual of handshaking was observed.

Pascal performed the introduction.

'*Je vous présente à Mademoiselle Mimette Florian—et Monsieur Gaston.*'

'*Enchanté,*' murmured the Saint, with a more than perfunctory intonation.

If three coincidences could seem to betray the machination of fate, then a fourth on top of them could be little short of an order from the gods. At any rate, the Saint was willing to accept it as that. For the last time he had seen the girl she had been driving a very different car, and had narrowly missed meeting him a lot sooner, in a very different atmosphere.

4

As with fine wines, fine food, and fine cars, the Saint's taste in fine-feathered birds was highly discriminating. This girl satisfied even his demanding standards.

'Lovely' is an overworked adjective. It is used to describe any pleasant experience from a holiday to a movie. Simon had little doubt that Mimette Florian would be an enjoyable experience, and none whatsoever that she lived up to the word's true definition of beautiful and attractive.

The mental picture he had carried with him since their near miss on the road paled beside the original. Her plain dress of green cotton

29

highlighted the grace of her figure without revealing it. She walked with the litheness of youth, but there was a confidence and authority about her that suggested a maturity beyond her years. Her hair curled as it touched her shoulders and framed a face that needed no cosmetics to enhance its appeal. But it was her eyes that held the Saint's attention. They were at the same time the wide wondering eyes of a child, and the dark secretive eyes of a worldly woman.

The man Gaston looked old enough to be her grandfather, but the way in which he waited for her to speak and stood a respectful half pace behind immediately stamped the relationship as one of employer and employee. Dressed in homespun breeches of oldfashioned cut, heavy workman's boots, and a black unbuttoned waistcoat over his striped shirt, he was the perfect prototype of a vanishing tradition of lifelong family retainer. Years of working in the open had burned his face to the colour and texture of worn leather, yet the lines that were the legacy of at least half a century of toil were offset by eyes that were as bright and clear as the sky.

The girl asked Pascal: 'What happened?'

Her voice was as devoid of emotion as if she had been asking the time. The Saint gave her full marks for self control.

Pascal rapidly explained how the Saint had

only been giving them a lift, and told her the story from the time they had spotted the smoke to how the Saint had rescued the truck. As he spoke of the two arsonists the old man's eyes glittered and his lips framed words he was too well trained to utter in the presence of a lady. Mimette listened calmly, the only sign of her thoughts being the compression of her lips and a hardening of her eyes. When Pascal had finished she turned to the Saint.

'We are in your debt, Monsieur. You must let us repay you for your trouble.'

She spoke as if she were addressing a tradesman who had performed a special favour, but her gaze held on the Saint's face and she seemed a little disconcerted by what she saw there.

Simon smiled and bowed with an air that was more mocking than obsequious and did more than any words could have done to take him out of the pigeonhole she had allotted him.

'My mother told me never to accept money from strange women,' he said solemnly. He spread out his hands so that the handkerchief wrapping was visible. 'But I'd be grateful for a chance to clean up and put something on this.'

'Why didn't you tell me the gentleman was hurt, Pascal?' she said sternly.

Before the youth could answer the Saint intervened, his face serious but his voice bantering.

31

'I've always fancied myself as the strong silent type but it is just a little painful.'

In fact it was not hurting too much, but he felt that the circumstances permitted a slight exaggeration. He had no intention of being patted on the head and sent on his way, when he had such a ready-made pretext for developing the acquaintance. And he had an idea that for all her attitude of stoical authority Mimette might prove a very sympathetic nurse.

Gaston told her almost too helpfully: 'If you want to take him to the château, *Mademoiselle*, I and the others will take care of everything here. Although there is really almost nothing to be done.'

The fire was too solidly established by then for amateur extinguishing. It would have to burn itself out until it exhausted the contents of the barn and failed to make an impression on the stone walls. Mimette saw the sense of the old man's words and sighed.

'Yes, I suppose you are right, Gaston,' she said, and there was more than a hint of tiredness in her voice. 'As you always are. Pascal and—?' She looked questioningly at the other student.

'Jules.'

'And Jules will help, too. Afterwards you will find them quarters with the other pickers.'

Gaston nodded.

'*Oui, Mademoiselle*.'

Simon showed Mimette the Hirondel.

'That is my car. Perhaps you would like to drive, since you know where we are going.'

'Thank you.'

She took the keys he held out as they walked over to the car.

'She's rather fierce on the throttle. Be careful how you put your foot down, or you might find you're where you were going before you realise you've started.'

His warning was answered with a withering look, and the Saint held up his hands in a pantomime of surrender.

'I'm sorry! I was forgetting that you know how to handle a car. But then if I hadn't braked so quickly I'd have had a new mascot for the bonnet.'

Her frown slowly dissolved into a smile.

'Of course! I was trying to remember where I had seen it before.' She examined the sleek lines of the Hirondel with evident approval. 'You were the man who nearly hit me.'

The Saint laughed as he held the door open for her.

'Actually I was under the impression that it was the other way round, but we won't labour the point.'

He climbed in and turned in his seat so that he could watch her. She started the engine and let in the clutch. After an initial kangaroo hop she handled the car competently enough.

They took the driveway down which the jeep

33

had come, towards the backdrop of buildings that he had not yet had time to sort out. The Saint admired her coolness, but it puzzled him. She could not have been much over twenty-one, but she had accepted the destruction of the barn and the threat it posed to the harvest without the dramatics he would have expected from someone of that age.

As they climbed the slope he was surprised to see that what had looked from below like the crest of an escarpment was in fact only the first of a series of hills set close together, each one topping the one before it. Only the dependencies which he had seen from the barn were actually on the first ridge: the château which overlooked them stood on the next hill, with a narrow valley between. Only an illusion of perspective had made its turrets and battlements seem to grow directly out of the nearer buildings.

Mimette seemed prepared to complete the trip in silence, but the Saint had no intention of wasting such an opportunity for conversation.

'I suppose you're getting hardened to disasters like this by now,' he remarked, as if he was just making an idle comment to pass the time.

'What do you know about the things that have been happening here?' said Mimette sharply.

'Only what Pascal told me on the drive here. That you've been having a lot of problems lately. Something about a curse.'

Mimette laughed scornfully.

'That is superstitious nonsense.'

'Of course,' Simon assented readily. 'There was certainly nothing ghostly about the two men who set fire to the barn. I know. I tackled one of them. I was amazed when my arm didn't go right through him.'

Mimette laughed again, and this time it was with genuine amusement.

'I'm quite sure they were real, just as all the other things that have happened have been done by real people and not the spooks the workers prefer to believe in.'

They had reached the foot of the valley and were climbing the second hill. In a few minutes they would reach the château and then it might be too late to gather all the information he wanted. There was no time for subtlety.

'What other things?'

'They are no concern of yours.'

'Perhaps not,' he agreed, but there was a new and harsher edge to his voice that she could not ignore. 'But I risked my skin to try and save your property. I think that entitles me to be curious.'

'Excuse me,' Mimette said penitently. 'I was very rude.'

'So what is the story?'

'It all started last year, shortly after the stone was dug up . . .'

'The stone?'

'Yes. A sort of tombstone. Very old and covered in ancient writing. One of the workmen discovered it when they were planting some new vines. Apparently it is some relic of the *Templiers*. They used to own the château.'

'Pascal told me about them.'

'Well, from then on things started happening. The vines we planted were sprayed with weedkiller. A few weeks later there was a fire in the pressing house, and a month after that my father was taken seriously ill with food poisoning. It's just gone on and on, one thing after another. Now nobody is surprised at anything that happens. The staff believe it is all to do with the stone. They say that it has awoken the Templars' curse. Some have even become so scared that they have left us.'

'And what do you believe, Mimette?' he asked gently.

He had been watching her as she talked and for the first time felt he had penetrated behind the mask of aloof efficiency.

The girl sighed.

'Quite honestly I don't know what to believe any more. Perhaps someone hates us enough to want the family bankrupted. Perhaps there really is a curse on the Florians. I really don't know.'

As they approached the château Simon surveyed it in more detail. It was exactly as

Pascal had described it, half mansion, half castle. The Saint had seen bigger and more grandiose châteaux in the Loire but never one more appropriate to its setting. There was at least four hundred years between the building of each element, yet they blended as harmoniously as if they had been designed by the same architect.

From where the driveway curved in front of it, the land rolled gently down to meet the fertile plain to the east through which a tributary river wound southwards on its way to join the Rhône. The remains of the walls of the ancient fortress ringed the site like a coronet. Made from stone hewn from the hillside and skilfully pieced together, they stretched from either side of an imposing gatehouse to completely enclose the château and the formal gardens behind it. The height of the wall varied; in some places it was twice the height of a man, in others only a few stones remained. The only part that appeared quite untouched by the centuries was a castellated tower in the west corner. It rose sheer for seventy feet, and the ivy that covered other sections of the wall appeared to have found no hold there.

The castle-mansion itself dominated the hilltop. The main central building of four storeys had clearly been restored from the old fortress, while the lower newer wings had been built with square sawn blocks of more modern

37

masonry. The Saint guessed that the château had developed from the original keep, and that the remains of the wall that ran straight across the hill in front of it would have served as the last line of defence. Perhaps it was there, he mused, that the Templars had made their final stand. It was the sort of place that made one think of knights and archers and sieges. As they drove past the massive base of the once-imposing towers of the gatehouse he would not have been surprised if d'Artagnan had swaggered out to greet them.

Between the remains of the inner wall and the château was a rectangular courtyard. Mimette drove across it and stopped in front of a flight of stone steps that swept up to a pair of high iron-studded double doors. Instead of d'Artagnan, a bent-backed major-domo who looked half as old as the house opened a door for them as they reached the top step. He had the appearance and the manner of someone who had been bowing and opening doors all his life, as impersonal as a portrait, listening to everything and hearing nothing.

'Thank you, Charles. You can bring some whisky to the small salon,' said Mimette, hardly glancing at him.

The butler bowed from the shoulders and shuffled off. The Saint looked around him and observed the simplicity of the hall. It was large and airy but almost bare. The floor was paved in plain white marble and a broad staircase of the same stone rose from the far end to serve a wooden gallery that ran around three sides of the hall. A few paintings of long-dead Florians hung in ornately gilded frames, and equally heavy armchairs stood against the walls on each side of the three doors that led off it. With the exception of a long trestle table in the centre and the large porcelain bowl that rested upon it, there was no other furniture.

The only other object of interest was a large rock shaped like a gravestone that stood in a recess by the stairs. It was covered with hieroglyphics.

As Simon sauntered towards it, the door on his left opened to admit a small man who would have seemed quite at home in the company of Snow White. He could not have been much more than five feet tall, and his lack of inches was not helped by a pair of rounded shoulders and a toddling kind of gait. His chubby face was as round as a full moon, and apart from a few tufts of white hair above his ears he was completely bald.

The new arrival wavered apologetically between the Saint and Mimette.

'Monsieur Norbert, this is...' She had to appeal to the Saint. 'I'm sorry, but you haven't told me your name.'

The Saint smiled. This, finally, was the moment of truth.

'So I haven't. And you're going to find it hard to believe. My name is Templar. Simon Templar.'

CHAPTER TWO

HOW CHARLES WAS
KEPT BUSY,
AND THE SAINT
SAW THE LIGHT

What's in a name? The answer depends on whether you have a nice euphonic one like William Shakespeare or were baptised Aloysius Codpiece. A rose by any other name may smell as sweet, but life would have been a lot harder for poets had it been called a cabbage.

The Saint considered Simon Templar a very satisfactory name and was always interested in the way others responded to it. The disclosure of his identity had been known to evoke a wide range of emotions, from apprehension among those with something to hide, through hatred among those who had cause to wish he had never been born, to blank indifference on the part of those whose reading of newspapers might be confined to the sports or fashion pages.

But on this unique occasion the reactions had to be something special.

Simon was prepared to enjoy the touch of melodrama which he had inevitably created, and he was not disappointed. Watching Mimette, he saw her stiffen as the name registered. The polite smile froze. Her eyes flashed with anger as her first instinct was to suspect him of making some insolent kind of joke.

'It's true,' he insisted softly. 'Would you like to see my passport?'

The blaze died out of her eyes, but they became hard and guarded as the mask of imperturbability slipped back into place.

'How interesting,' she remarked with calculated indifference.

'Interesting! It is more than interesting,' Norbert exclaimed, and the Saint regarded him with renewed curiosity.

He had not ignored the little man's reaction and had noticed the drooping shoulders straighten and the new light that sparkled in the prominent fish-like eyes at the word Templar.

'Monsieur Norbert is an authority on the Templars,' Mimette stated flatly. 'He is professor of medieval history at the Sorbonne and is here to try to decipher the inscription on the stone.'

'It's a pleasure to meet you,' said the Saint cordially, and held out his hand.

Norbert grasped it between both fleshy palms and shook it as if trying to draw water from a pump.

41

'And to meet you. I would like to talk with you at length,' he enthused. 'Do you know your genealogy? How far back can you trace your family? You have almost no accent, but perhaps an *émigré* family after the Revolution? Yes?'

The Saint winced and retrieved his hand to readjust the handkerchief wrapping. He appeared to consider the questions seriously for a moment.

'A fellow called Adam on my father's side and a lady named Eve on my mother's. We haven't gone beyond that yet,' he replied brightly.

Mimette stepped between them with the adroitness of a cocktail party hostess disengaging two incompatible guests.

'Monsieur Templar is hurt,' she explained. 'I was about to tend to his injury.' She turned back to the Saint. 'This way, please.'

She began to climb the stairs and the Saint made to follow her, but Norbert grabbed his arm.

'I am sorry. But you touch on my obsession. Another time, perhaps?'

The Saint disengaged his sleeve as deftly as possible. He had an unreasonable prejudice against men with damp clutching hands.

'Certainly,' he acceded pleasantly. 'I always wondered how great-great-grandfather made it to England without his head.'

Before the earnest professor could relaunch his attack the Saint had joined Mimette at the top of the stairs. When he looked back Norbert was kneeling beside the stone, with lines of intense concentration furrowing his brow as he scribbled in a small notebook.

'What a character!' commented the Saint, shaking his head in discreet ambiguity.

'Oh, he's very harmless,' Mimette said. 'Quite sweet really when he isn't going on about the Templars, which is ninety per cent of the time.'

'Where did you find him?'

'We didn't. He found us. He was in charge of an archaeological dig at Orange when he heard about the stone. He was so excited that he came over and my father asked him to stay for a few days. He has practically lived here ever since.'

'If he hangs around till Christmas you could always put him on top of the tree,' Simon suggested helpfully, but the smile faded from Mimette's lips and her eyes clouded over again.

'If we are still here at Christmas,' she said wryly, and then, as if regretting her words, quickened her steps briskly.

Simon followed her in silence around the balcony and along a passage leading off to the right. He wondered how long it would take to qualify as a guide to the château. The old house appeared to have been built to no specific plan, as if the rooms had been added haphazardly when and where they were needed. The result was a confusing obstacle course of corridors and staircases. All he could tell of their destination was that it lay somewhere towards the rear of the château in the east wing. After some abrupt turns and arbitrary changes of level they passed through a vast echoing gallery panelled with more stiffly posed portraits, presumably of Florian forebears, before descending to ground level again via a more modern flight of wooden stairs. They met no one and heard nothing but the sound of their own footsteps. After the sunlit spaciousness of its outdoors the interior of the château seemed oppressive, almost claustrophobic.

Finally Mimette stopped and ushered the Saint into a small sitting-room. It was comfortably furnished with the sort of heavily upholstered Napoleonic sofas that were designed to relax on rather than to admire. In contrast with the other areas that he had seen, it was a room that was obviously lived in, the kind that is found behind doors marked Private in stately homes and is a mile removed from the imposing suites with their Louis XV and Chippendale which are on show to the paying public. A pair of plain glass doors opened on to a patio, beyond which was a neatly clipped lawn that stretched between banks of flowering shrubs to the remains of the castle's outer walls. In the centre was an ancient well that might have once served the beleaguered knights.

Mimette told him that she would not be long

and left. The Saint stretched himself full length on a sofa from which he could look out of the window and thought over the events of the previous hours.

His involvement had happened so swiftly, through a chain of circumstances that no solvent bookmaker would have laid odds about, that he felt slightly like a canoeist who had been pitched into the centre of the rapids and now, between rocks, could take advantage of a lull to study the river around him.

It was, to say the least, an intriguing situation. A noble family plagued by a curse that was being helped to work by a couple of small-time crooks. A proud and beautiful young woman too well aware of her station to show her emotions openly, but most certainly a very frightened female. A magnificent house that had about it a feeling of foreboding as if even the walls were waiting for something to happen. Plus, for good measure, a professor trying to understand some sort of primitive tombstone. It was like a crossword puzzle with only half the clues and no black squares.

It was, as Mimette had so bluntly pointed out, no business of his; but if the Saint had always minded his own business there would have been very few stories to write about him.

'The game's afoot,' he quoted to the pleasant garden he was staring at. 'But what's the game?'

He was still no nearer to an answer when

Mimette returned carrying a tray on which were a bowl of hot water, a jar of pink ointment, and a roll of gauze. The Saint rolled up the right sleeve of his shirt and removed his improvised bandage.

Mimette held his hand and carefully bathed his blackened palm. When she had cleaned it she looked up at him sharply.

'This burn is really almost nothing,' she accused.

'That's what I thought,' he said shamelessly.

'Then why did you—?'

'But it was a wonderful excuse to spend more time with you, and to have you hold my hand.'

She released the hand quickly as an elderly lady in a black dress that bulged in all the wrong places entered with the whisky, a siphon, and glasses. The Saint guessed that she was the spouse of the retainer who had opened the door for them. If possible she was even more self-effacing than her husband. She placed the silver salver on a table beside the sofa and left without a word. Mimette never even looked at her and the Saint's smile of thanks went unnoticed.

'I ought to have you thrown out,' Mimette said as the door closed.

'Why didn't you?' Simon concurred helpfully.

'Because I am beginning to think I have heard your name before.'

'And you think I might be a distant relative—

or too much for Charles to handle?'

Her eyes searched his face.

'You are called the Saint, *n'est-ce pas*?'

'By some people. But what are you afraid of?'

His question was intentionally ambiguous, but her first choice of answers was not the one that he was aiming for.

'You are a pirate. You rob people. They say you have even murdered some.'

'"Pirate" sounds so much nicer than "thief". Thank you,' he replied calmly. 'Though I suppose whichever word you use it comes to the same thing. But I've never robbed anyone who didn't deserve it, and there are some people who are enormously improved by death.'

Mimette poured out one liberal Scotch and a token spoonful in the other glass. The Saint sipped his drink and allowed her time to marshal her thoughts. When she finally spoke her voice was husky and uncertain.

'I must not forget that at this moment we are in your debt. But what do you really want from us?'

'Well, as you can see, even if I'm not critically injured, I got myself a bit messed up. If you felt truly hospitable, you'd offer me a bath and a chance to change my clothes.'

As soon as the words were out he cursed himself for his casualness. Mimette rose at once and pulled a bell sash. She did not return to her seat but walked to the window and stood with

47

her back to him looking out across the lawn.

'Mimette,' he said gently, 'believe me, I want nothing from you or your family. It was purely an accident that brought me here. Or a whim of fate. But I know now that you're in trouble. I might be able to help. I'd like to if you'd let me. But you would have to trust me. Could you trust me?'

The Saint concentrated every ounce of his personality into his voice, speaking his words of reassurance quietly but firmly, staying where he was rather than pressurising the girl by moving closer.

For a full minute she continued to stare out into the garden, until at last she turned and met his eyes. When she spoke there was a strange weariness behind her response.

'Why not? What have I got to lose?'

She walked slowly back to the sofa and sat down.

'I'm not sure where to start. It all seems so inexplicable. Someone is trying to make us bankrupt, to force us to leave Ingare. I think...'

But the Saint was not yet to know what she thought. The rap of a discreet knock and the opening of the door made her stop abruptly, as the manservant entered.

Mimette stood up, becoming once again the ice-blooded mistress of the house.

'Charles, will you take Monsieur Templar to a

guest room and run a bath for him? When he is ready, show him to the main salon.'

The servant held the door open and there was nothing for Simon to do but go with him. With a parting nod to Mimette he turned and trailed the major-domo up to the second floor and through another minor labyrinth to the chamber assigned to him.

The Saint wondered about the daffodil painted on the centre of the door but its significance became apparent as soon as he entered the room. It was completely decorated in various shades of yellow. Curtains, carpet, bedspread were all pale gold, while the chairs were upholstered in a lemon-coloured velvet. Even the wardrobe doors were painted with yellow panels. Simon stood for a moment taking it all in.

'The only thing it needs is a canary,' he observed drily.

'In the old days when servants were illiterate it was found convenient to identify rooms by colour rather than numbers or letters, sir,' Charles explained with the practised fluency of one used to providing the information.

The Saint crossed to the window and looked out while the servant ran his bath. Immediately in front of him was a curved balcony which jutted out over the remains of the castle wall that ran from the château to the tower. From the tower the rear wall ran almost to the other end of the house before meeting a huddle of one-level outbuildings that undoubtedly served for pressing and vatting the wine. Below them would be a series of cellars where the wine would be bottled and stored.

The servant returned from the adjoining bathroom and asked: 'Can I help you undress, m'sieu?'

'No, thank you,' said the Saint. 'But perhaps you would fetch my valise from the car.'

He handed over the car keys and waited until Charles had gone before starting to remove his shirt. It was not that he was bashful about undressing in front of a stranger, but he had no wish to excite comment, and the six-inch throwing knife strapped to his left forearm would certainly have done just that. After hiding the sheath under a pillow he hung up his clothes and walked through to the bathroom, which was an anachronistic conversion to ultra-modern plumbing.

It was full of steam, and he opened the window to let it out. The sight that greeted him made him step quickly back and stand very still.

On the track that led from the castle down towards the river was parked a black Citroën identical to the one he had seen beside the burning barn, and walking towards it from the tower were two men whose shapes he clearly recognised even at that distance.

In a movie, Simon Templar would have leapt from the window on to the balcony below, then swung like Errol Flynn across to the battlements, and after running along the crumbling catwalk would have dived like an avenging angel on to the two unsuspecting miscreants. In real life, the Saint stayed where he was and watched.

It was not that he lacked the athletic agility and strength to perform the required gymnastics. The main restraining factor was that he wanted to win the confidence of the Florian family, and such trust is not normally given to guests who leap stark naked from bathroom windows and jump on other men, however laudable their motives. There was also the equally practical consideration that they might well have gone away before he could reach them.

The men were climbing into their car when a third figure ran from the tower and pressed a package into the hands of the smaller of the other two. The combination of angle and distance prevented the Saint from getting anything more than a fleeting glimpse of the newcomer before he turned back and was again hidden by the tower.

The Citroën turned and accelerated away down the track. Simon did not waste time following its route but instead focused his attention on the tower. For several minutes he maintained his vigil but the third man did not reappear. The Saint was disappointed but realised that his view of anyone leaving the tower by an outside door would have been screened by the walls.

When it was obvious that he was not likely to see any more, he lowered himself into the no longer scalding water and pondered every detail of what he had witnessed. There was a deduction to be made, but it only added to his collection of question marks.

The major-domo returned, and came as far as the bathroom door.

'I have brought your valise, m'sieu. Do you wish me to unpack it?'

'*Non, merci*,' Simon said. 'I'd prefer to find what I want.'

'If you ring the bell when you are ready, m'sieu, I will come and show you to the principal salon.'

'Thank you.'

'*A votre service*.'

Service was a fine thing, Simon reflected, but he could soon have too much of it.

When he had completed his ablutions and dried himself, he returned to the bedroom and found his suitcase on a stool beside the bed. As he bent to unlock it he could not help looking out of the window at the panorama now suffused with the rosy tints of approaching sunset into which the Citroën had disappeared; he remembered how the third man had returned towards the tower and had not been sighted again.

The inescapable conclusion was that he had come into the château. And was probably still inside. And very possibly had been all along.

An illuminating corollary was that there had been no attempt to hide the Citroën even though it could have been seen by anybody looking out of a window on the second or third storey. Which suggested that the accomplice was in a position to account for his actions if challenged, or that he knew the whereabouts of everyone else in the house.

'But how corny it would be,' Simon told his reflection in the mirror as he combed his hair, 'to have the faithful old butler be the villain...'

To replace the garments which had suffered the dishevelment of his salvage efforts, he selected an extravagantly patterned shirt from Nassau, a pair of light blue slacks, and a featherweight jacket. The combination restored the image of a disarmingly relaxed vacationing tourist which, in essence, was exactly what he was.

He ignored the bell pull that would have summoned the major-domo to show him to the drawing-room and quietly turned the door handle and slipped out into the deserted corridor. His action might be frowned upon by his hostess and would certainly scandalise the worthy Charles, but he had had enough of being shepherded for a while, and he felt like doing a little exploring on his own. He reasoned that if he was found anywhere he should not be he had the perfect excuse of being lost in a strange house—which, he mused as he remembered the maze of passages, he probably would be.

He was able to retrace the route the servant had taken until he arrived at the right-angled turn-off of a narrow corridor which seemed to connect the east wing with the main body of the château. He had a feeling that if there was anything to be discovered during his wandering it would be in the older section of the house.

Inside the main building, the corridor abruptly became a much wider passage, lit by a tall window at the far end. From the number of doors along either side, it appeared to bisect the building, giving access to both front and back rooms.

The Saint moved swiftly along it, making less noise than a stalking cat. He opened doors at random, but found nothing more exciting than bedrooms and an occasional cupboard or lumber room.

The end of the passage, by the tall window there, proved to be also a landing for a spiral stone staircase leading both upwards and downwards. Judging that the upper floor would be no more exciting than the one he was on, he took the stairs down to the first floor, which turned out to be an equally barren hunting ground. The only room of any interest was a large well-stocked library that would have taken far too long to search.

The main problem, he conceded, as he found himself looking down another corridor leading to the balcony around the entrance hall, was that he had no idea what he was hoping to find. He was simply gambling on blind luck to produce something.

He glanced at his watch and was surprised to see that well over an hour had passed since he had left Mimette. He could not delay much longer, or Charles would be coming to look for him, whether summoned or not. He was considering whether to abandon his quest when he heard a door slam and the sound of footsteps coming along the balcony towards the corridor.

On impulse he stepped back on to the spiral staircase and continued down it. The steps became steeper with every turn, and he expected that they would eventually lead to a basement, perhaps even to the original dungeons of the castle. Instead, they ended on the ground floor, but from the way they twisted towards a blank wall they must have once carried on down to the foundations. A padlocked door in the wall facing the final step had pointedly been installed to restrict entrance to the cellars.

It was evident that he had reached the oldest

part of the château. A bare stone passage with a low ceiling of tiny red bricks ran from the foot of the stairway into what had once been the great hall of the castle. The room was vast compared to the others he had visited, being at least eighty feet long and almost half as many wide. The ceiling was made of planks the width of the trees they had been cut from, and broad shafts of fading light slanted down from a dozen arched windows set high up in the wall. Except for a few faded tapestries and a couple of roughly carpentered trestle tables it was completely empty. The entrance from the passage was in the centre of the hall, an equal distance from two doors which were the only other breaks in the flat lines of the walls.

Simon considered each in turn as he weighed his next move. The more imposing of the two was set in the wall which he estimated to be nearest the centre of the château, while the one at the east end of the hall was much smaller and half hidden in a recess. Of the two, the smaller looked the more intriguing but he was acutely aware that time was not on his side. Regretfully he turned towards the main door which, he guessed, would take him in the general direction of the reception hall and, very likely, the salon.

It was then that he heard the voices. They were so faint that had it not been for the complete stillness that surrounded him and his own finely tuned hearing he would never have noticed them. At first he thought they must be coming from a long way off, but then he realised that the walls were too thick to admit any outside noise short of a trumpet call. He walked into the centre of the hall and stood completely motionless as he strained to locate the source of the sound. He tried putting a hand over each ear in turn. The noise was completely blotted out when he covered his right ear. With a smile he turned towards the smaller of the two doors.

The voices grew slightly stronger as he approached but they were still far too muffled for him to distinguish any words. In vain he tried pressing his ear against the door. Following the only course left, he turned the iron ring handle. The door was still immovable. Keeping hold of the handle, he rapped it against the woodwork. Instantly the voices ceased.

The thickness of the door allowed only the vaguest sounds of movement to penetrate its stout timbers. He knocked again and waited impatiently until a bolt scraped in its channel and the door creaked open six inches to reveal the frowning countenance of Professor Norbert.

'Oh, it's you,' said the Saint pleasantly, but he received no answering smile from the scholar.

'What do you want?' Norbert asked curtly.

The Saint disliked conversations carried on through furtively half-opened doors.

'I'm lost,' he informed the professor

innocently, and pushed the door wider.

The question of whether the little man wanted the Saint to enter was as academic as one of his own textbooks. Simon intended to gain admission, and simply applied the necessary pressure to the object that impeded his progress. Norbert took a startled step backwards, and the Saint smiled apologetically.

'I hope I'm not disturbing your devotions.'

'My devotions? Oh, yes, I see what you mean,' stammered the flustered professor as he followed the Saint's gaze.

Simon took in the details of his surroundings quickly and expertly. He noted the whitewashed walls and the fluted stone pillars that supported the vaulted ceiling. He took account of the rows of elaborately carved pews and the impressive brass eagle lectern. He admired the stained glass of the windows, the workmanship that had gone into the silver cross and candlesticks on the altar, and the delicate carving of the effigies of a knight and his lady who lay on top of an ornate tomb in the alcove beside it. And he came to the conclusion that the only people now in the chapel were himself and Norbert.

'This isn't Vosges, is it?' he enquired.

'I'm sorry, I do not understand.'

'Like St. Joan, I kept hearing voices,' Simon explained.

The professor managed a hesitant smile.

'Another of your jokes, Monsieur Templar?

All you can have heard is me.'

'Talking to yourself? Do you do that a lot?'

'I was reading the inscription on the tomb. I often read aloud. It helps me remember,' said the professor testily. 'Would you like to look at it?'

The Saint shook his head.

'Not right now, but I would like to look at the salon. As I said, I'm lost.'

Norbert walked past him and beckoned him to follow.

'Come, I will show you the way.'

'Do forgive me for disturbing you,' Simon drawled.

He walked through the hall behind his guide. Norbert led the way to the larger door, which opened into the reception area, across to a small anteroom, and through that into the salon.

As the Saint entered, two men rose to greet him. There was no sign of Mimette.

Norbert performed the introductions.

'Monsieur Templar, Philippe Florian, Henri Pichot.'

The Saint shook hands with each in turn as he proffered the conventional greetings. Norbert mumbled an excuse and left.

Florian was a tall sturdily built man in his early forties who looked as if he had once been an athlete but had allowed the muscles of youth to become the flab of middle age. He wore a grey lounge suit that was a shade too sharply tailored. His black hair was pomaded straight back and he sported a thin moustache that did not reach the corners of his mouth. Despite the firmness of his handshake and the direct appraising look that he bestowed on his guest there was something about him that reminded the Saint of an overfed lizard.

His companion was a good fifteen years younger and a head shorter, and whereas Florian radiated an aura of authority Pichot seemed continually nervous and ill at ease. The frankness of his clean-shaven features seemed to conceal an inner uncertainty, which also characterised his clothes. He wore a tweed sports coat and flannels but combined them with a stiff-collared white shirt and staid dark blue tie.

Simon addressed himself to Florian.

'You must be Mimette's father.'

'Her uncle,' Florian corrected him. 'And you are the hero of the day, I understand.'

'Am I?' said the Saint deprecatingly.

'Indeed you are,' Florian boomed.

He seemed to be incapable of saying anything quietly or of not beaming when he talked. The Saint found neither mannerism as friendly or as reassuring as it was intended.

'I've heard all about your efforts to save the barn, and I can't tell you how grateful we are,' Florian continued. 'To lose the equipment is an inconvenience, but had we lost the truck it would have been a catastrophe.'

'Where is Mimette?' Simon asked in an attempt to steer the conversation away from his heroism.

Florian appeared irritated at having his speech interrupted.

'She apologises for not being here. She has gone to see what can be bought or borrowed from the neighbouring farms to make good what we lost this afternoon. One hopes she will be able to get what is needed.'

'Baskets and hand carts are not impossible to replace,' Pichot explained, 'but there is never a vehicle to be hired around here at harvest time. Our *récolte* begins tomorrow, so you see how important it is.'

'Mimette tells me you won't hear of a reward, but I want you to know we shall never forget your help. Any time you are in the district you must come and see us. I'm so sorry that our troubles have delayed your journey.' Florian crossed to the bell pull and operated it vigorously.

'Oh, it livened up the afternoon,' Simon remarked carelessly, and had hardly finished speaking before the door opened and the major-domo carried in his valise.

'When Charles found that you had left your room, he took the liberty of packing your things. I hope you don't mind.'

The Saint kept his face serenely impassive

and awarded the match to Florian on points. He appreciated expertise in any field, and he could not have faulted the way Florian was performing the smoothest and most genteel example of the bum's rush.

'How kind of him,' he replied coldly, but made no move to pick up the suitcase.

'Charles will carry it to your car,' Pichot said hastily, in some embarrassment. 'We are desolated to have delayed your journey for so long.'

The butler picked up the valise, and the Saint followed him out through the marble hall and down the steps outside to the Hirondel. Pichot and Florian walked a pace behind him. Had they been carrying a brace of .38s they could not have made a slicker job of marching him out.

The Saint opened the rear lid and got in to the driving seat. He fired the engine, keeping his foot on the accelerator while he readjusted the seat which Mimette had pushed forward when she drove. Then he got out again, leaving the engine to warm up while he verified the stowage of his suitcase. He thanked Charles, closed the hatch, and got in again behind the wheel.

All the time his brain was flailing around for any pretext that would keep him there until Mimette returned, or give him a reason to return and see her very soon. No matter what, he was determined that their last conversation should not remain unfinished.

And then the temperature gauge on the dashboard caught his eye. The needle was hovering well inside the red danger zone. The engine coughed and misfired.

He quickly switched off the ignition and climbed out. He walked to the front of the car and opened it. One long look told him that the Hirondel would be going nowhere that evening. In the centre of the radiator was a hole the size of an apple. No stone thrown up from the road could have caused such damage.

The Saint tried not to smile as he straightened up. It was simple, crude, but very effective sabotage.

3

The Saint was extremely fond of his car and at any other time would have been dangerously angry with the perpetrator of such vandalism. At that moment however he felt only a genuine gratitude to the mysterious saboteur. No Hirondel equalled no immediate departure, and the pleasure the equation gave him was considerably increased by the anticipation of the annoyance it would cause to the two men waiting impatiently to wave him farewell.

Florian and Pichot had hurried down the steps as soon as he began to peer at the engine. He ignored them while he checked thoroughly for any other signs of damage. Finally satisfied that the radiator had been the only target, he turned to face them.

'What is wrong?' Florian demanded with a passable imitation of genuine concern.

Simon stepped aside and pointed, so that both men could see for themselves. Florian coloured slightly as the significance of the damage registered. Pichot shuffled his feet and looked uneasily from the car to the Saint and back to the car.

'It must have happened during the drive from the barn,' Simon theorised, in simulated dismay. 'It seems to be an unlucky day, I'm afraid.'

'Can you mend it?' Pichot asked anxiously.

The Saint shook his head.

'Not a hope. The whole radiator will have to be replaced.'

'How inconvenient,' Florian muttered, more to himself than the Saint, but added quickly: 'for you.'

'Yes, isn't it?' Simon agreed.

They looked steadily at each other, each of them blandly declining to admit that anything remained unspoken.

Sensing the latent hostility building up between them, Pichot stepped forward, speaking first to Florian and then to the Saint.

'Let us go back into the house. I will telephone the local garage and see what can be done.'

'Good idea,' Simon seconded agreeably. 'You

64

never know, they might be able to help.'

He knew that they would not, but the attempt would help prolong his leave-taking. The Hirondel was no ordinary production-line car, and he was confident that it would be impossible to fit a radiator from any other make. The nearest Hirondel agents were in Nice, but if they had a spare in stock it would take time to deliver.

Pichot ran up the steps and disappeared into the château. Florian summoned up some of his former bonhomie and even went so far as to give the Saint a reassuring pat on the back as they walked back to the drawing-room.

'I'm sure we shall be able to do something. We might even be able to hire a car while yours is being repaired.'

'I thought you said it was impossible to hire anything at vintage time,' the Saint reminded him gently.

'Yes, well, I was thinking of lorries and tractors. It might be easier to arrange a car to take you where you were going.'

'Honestly, it's not serious,' Simon assured him. 'I wasn't going anywhere special.'

'You are being too generous. But it is our responsibility.'

Florian was clearly on edge and sounded as if he was trying to convince himself more than the Saint. As they entered the salon Simon noted with satisfaction that the clock stood at nearly

6.30. They would certainly have to pull out all the stops if they were going to shift him that evening. Henri Pichot was not there, doubtless trying his pull.

Florian opened a corner cabinet to reveal several well stocked shelves.

'Would you care for a Scotch?'

'Thank you.'

This was the beginning of a new era when the traditional *apéritifs* had lost ground in fashionable French circles, and whisky had become the snob before-dinner drink among those who aspired to be up to date.

Florian poured for both of them, added soda and ice from an insulated bucket in the cupboard, and said: *'Chin.'*

'Chin.'

Another Anglo-American importation.

The Saint relaxed in an armchair and sipped his drink appreciatively. The Scotch was, as he would have expected, of the finest quality, a twelve-year-old malt.

'I understand you've been having a lot of trouble lately,' he said conversationally.

Florian shrugged and spread out his hands in an exaggerated gesture of resignation.

'A few misfortunes, certainly, but one must expect these things in any business. And running a vineyard is a business, even if my brother does not consider it so.'

'I should have thought that people setting fire

to buildings and spraying vines with weedkiller were hardly ordinary business hazards,' Simon remarked. Anticipating a question, he added: 'Mimette told me about that.'

Florian threw back half his Scotch in one go. He rotated the tumbler between his palms as he glanced furtively at the clock.

'Ah, Mimette. I see.' He made a long pause. 'Poor girl, she takes life so seriously for one so young. Since her mother died last year she has had a lot of new responsibilities to cope with. My brother is not the most worldly of men. I think the English refer to such people as "one of the old school". Mimette has helped to run the château and the vineyard, and I'm afraid the strain is telling. She tends to over-dramatise things. Sometimes I wonder if it is not becoming an obsession.'

It was a clever speech. Without a single disloyal word, he had managed to praise and raise doubts about his brother and his niece at the same time. Philippe Florian might be pompous but he was certainly shrewd. And he was worried, far more so than Mimette had been earlier that afternoon.

'Better to be obsessed than sit by and watch your family ruined!'

The Saint and Florian turned simultaneously as the girl's voice cut between them. She stood framed in the doorway, her hair windblown from the drive and a red glow flaming her cheeks.

'Ah, *vous voici*,' Simon exclaimed, springing to his feet. 'I was afraid I was going to miss you.'

'I apologise for having to leave you to the company of Uncle Philippe,' she said, 'but there has been a lot to do. For those of us who work, that is.'

Mimette turned angrily towards her uncle, but he appeared only tolerantly amused by the barb she had flung at him.

'You'll be sorry to hear that I've managed to get everything we need. Gaston worked wonders as usual. Papa is writing the cheques. He'll be with us shortly.'

'Now why should I be sorry, Mimette?' Florian demurred suavely. 'You really must stop thinking of me as the wicked uncle in a fairy tale.'

Mimette sank into a chair and took a cigarette from the silver box on the coffee table. She lit it and inhaled deeply, letting out the smoke like a long sigh.

'Wicked half-uncle,' she corrected coldly, and Florian looked pained. 'And I only wish you would stop acting like one. Whenever anything goes wrong, there's good old Philippe lending money and patting everyone on the back and telling them not to worry, and all the time scheming to take control and kick out everyone else.'

'Helping one's brother, even one's half-brother as you insist on pointing out, is not something discreditable. And as for scheming, I don't call making a generous offer to buy Ingare scheming. I call it business. Producing and selling wine is an industry, not a pastime, and if you all realised that then you might still be able to salvage something from the mess you've got yourselves into.'

For the first time Simon had proof of the hardness he had always suspected behind Florian's urbane façade. He sipped his drink and did his best to fade into the background as he listened to the exchange. It was as edifying as any eavesdropping could be.

Philippe's partial explosion was followed by an oppressive silence like the hush before a thunderstorm, and the Saint waited for the clouds to burst. But the protocols of good breeding and dirty-linen-washing prevailed. Florian downed the dregs of his drink but made no move to replenish his glass. And then the telephone shattered the stillness and the moment was lost.

Mimette jumped up and strode across the room to snatch up the receiver. She listened for a few moments and then gently replaced it in its cradle. She turned to the Saint.

'That was the garage. They say they will not be able to send anyone to look at your car until tomorrow. What is wrong with it?'

'The radiator is holed. Henri was trying to get

69

it fixed for me.'

'I saw him heading for the *chai* as I drove up. He must have switched the call through to here in case they phoned back while he was out. What will you do now?'

'I don't know. I wouldn't get more than two hundred metres before the engine seized. What's the hotel situation like around here?'

'A hotel? Don't be ridiculous,' said Mimette. 'We wouldn't hear of such a thing. Of course, you will stay here.'

'After what you have done for us, that is the least we can offer,' said Philippe warmly.

Simon had to admire the man's ability to react so quickly to events. The about-face was so complete that a doubt about his assessment even entered the Saint's suspicious mind.

'But that's giving you too much trouble,' he protested hypocritically.

'Not at all,' boomed Philippe, as if there had never been any question of an alternative in his mind.

He rang the bell and the major-domo entered so quickly that he must have been standing within feet of the door.

'Charles, please take Monsieur Templar's valise back to his room. He will be staying to dinner.'

'*Oui, m'sieu.*'

Once again the Saint handed over his car keys. When Charles had left the salon Simon said: 'I'm afraid I'm giving him a lot to do. Is it a problem to get staff so far out in the country?'

'We have only Charles and his wife living in. There are two others who come in daily.' Mimette sighed. 'When I was a little girl we kept a whole army of servants here, but we can no longer afford them.'

'Still longing for the good old days,' scoffed Philippe Florian. To the Saint he said: 'I must tidy myself up a little. You will join us again for another drink in, perhaps, three-quarters of an hour?' He stalked briskly from the room, and Simon looked at Mimette hopefully.

'Can we continue our talk?'

'There's not much more to tell,' she replied, and once again he noted the tiredness in her voice.

He felt very sorry for her. In one respect at least he agreed with her uncle. She might well be taking her responsibilities a little too seriously.

She stubbed out her cigarette with a vindictiveness that displayed the depth of her struggle to control her emotions.

'We are in serious financial trouble. Philippe wants to own the château, more importantly he wants to own us. He has always been jealous of my father. He hates the fact that Ingare came to my father and not to him. That he is not regarded as a true Florian.'

'But surely he is a fully paid-up member of

71

the family, even if he is only your father's half-brother?'

'There is more to being a member of a family than just being tied to people by blood,' Mimette retorted fiercely.

'I'm sorry, I don't understand.'

Mimette picked up another cigarette, fiddled with it aimlessly for a moment, and then crushed it in her hand. She brushed the debris from her hands into the empty grate. She looked intently at the Saint, a sarcastic smile curling her lips.

'You are not the only one. Philippe does not understand anything. That some people have long memories. Or that if it were not for my father he would long ago have been a dead man.'

'I give up,' said the Saint, not too patiently. 'What's the answer?'

'Perhaps I will tell you soon—I must have time to think.' Mimette seemed to wonder if she had already said too much, and to be glad of an excuse to back away again. 'Now I must get dressed for dinner. Shall I have Charles show you back to your room?'

'I think I can find my own way now,' said the Saint.

'*Alors, à toute à l'heure.*'

While he changed into the plain dark suit which he assumed would be expected of him, he reviewed the events of the day and came up with practically nothing but riddles.

Mimette's outburst added another dimension to the picture he had been building up, but it was pointless to try to guess the dark secrets she was hinting at. The episode in the chapel was another mystery: he had great faith in the efficiency of his senses, and whatever the professor might say, he knew that he had heard two people talking. And finally there was the sabotage of his car: while Philippe and Pichot had seemed palpably eager to speed him on his way, someone else was trying even harder to keep him there.

A knock at the door put an end to his reverie and brought Charles into the room.

'Monsieur Philippe asked me to show you to the dining-room, m'sieu.'

'Very well,' said the Saint resignedly. 'I'll follow you.'

The dining-room turned out to be at the rear of the house behind the salon. It was furnished with some of the best examples of Empire furniture the Saint had seen outside the captivity of museums. The wall on the garden side was composed almost completely of glass doors, firmly closed against the refreshing coolness of the night air. Along the centre of the room was a table capable of seating twenty with space to spare. The seven places set around one end looked almost insignificant.

Five people turned to greet him. All except one he had already met, and the fifth could only be the half-brother of Philippe Florian. Mimette introduced him as her father, Yves.

At sixty the master of Ingare looked older than Simon had expected, but age had not bowed him even if it had left its mark on his face. He matched the Saint for height, and unlike his brother carried no excess weight. Simon could see where Mimette had inherited her looks, and reckoned that Florian had been more than averagely handsome in his youth. Now his face was deeply lined around tired eyes, and what had once been a lean face had become gaunt, but his handshake was strong and his smile was unquestionably genuine as he welcomed his guest.

'It is a pleasure to meet you, Monsieur Templar. I have heard everything you did for us. I am very grateful.'

'It was very little, and the damage to my car was not your fault,' Simon disclaimed.

Yves Florian offered a drink from the row of bottles on the sideboard, and Mimette told him: 'I think Monsieur Templar should stay for a few days. I'm sure he would be interested to watch the start of the wine-making.'

'I should be delighted,' Yves responded cordially.

Philippe turned quickly away and poured himself another Scotch from the bottle beside him.

Yves indicated the others in the room.

'I understand you have already met Henri Pichot. May I present his uncle, Gaston Pichot. Gaston is our overseer, taster, chief blender, and hardest worker and without him Ingare would crumble overnight.'

The old man coloured slightly at his employer's praise. He stepped forward and shook the Saint's hand. He seemed as ill at ease in his carefully pressed black suit as he had been comfortable in his working clothes in the fields that afternoon.

'It's nice to see you again,' said the Saint. 'We met at the barn this afternoon.'

Over the sideboard hung a full length portrait of a tall handsome man dressed in the extravagant frippery of the late eighteenth century. There was a quality about the rakish features and insolent hand on hilt stance that appealed to the Saint. Still groping for any sort of information, he used it as a cue to remark: 'He must be another Florian—I can see a family resemblance.'

'That was the Baron Robert,' Gaston informed him, with reflected pride.

'It's a striking portrait.'

'And a striking man, though his contemporaries would not have agreed,' Philippe put in. 'They thought him a traitor for supporting the Revolution.'

'And keeping his head when all his friends were losing theirs,' added Mimette cynically.

'Not only did he survive the Terror but Napoleon made him a general.'

'How long has Ingare been in your family?' was the natural question.

'Since soon after the Templars left,' Yves replied. 'I have read that in 1305 a certain Esquiu de Floyran of Béziers offered to betray "the secrets of the Templars", whatever they may have been, first to James the Second of Aragon, and then to King Philippe of France. To force the Pope's hand, Philippe was able to denounce the Templars to the Inquisition, since the Grand Inquisitor was his personal confessor and protégé. In 1307 the arrest of the Templars began. It is thought that Floyran may have received Ingare as part of his reward, and that the name "Florian" was derived from his.'

'One sees the family resemblance to Baron Robert,' observed Mimette acidly.

'Who knows what reasons people may have had, so many centuries ago?' said Yves good-humouredly.

Charles came in to announce that dinner was ready, and there was a move towards the dining table.

Yves Florian took the head of it, and seated the Saint on his right and Mimette on his left. Philippe was placed next to Mimette, Gaston and Henri next to the Saint. As he unfolded his serviette, Yves looked at the empty seat beside Philippe and frowned.

'And where is our worthy professor this evening?' he wondered.

'Still prospecting, I suppose,' said Mimette and the others laughed at what was clearly a standing joke.

While Mrs Charles, as Simon had dubbed the major-domo's wife, wheeled in a trolley with a large serving platter of *truites amandine* and hot plates which she proceeded to distribute, Norbert entered. He apologised for his lateness and sat down.

'Any luck today?' Mimette asked pleasantly.

The professor regarded her as he might have regarded an impudent student.

'It is not a question of luck but of knowledge and application,' he said primly.

'Then we can be sure you will succeed if you only have enough time,' Henri said with studiously veiled sarcasm.

Mrs Charles brought the platter to each place in turn for the guests to help themselves, while Charles himself circulated with a bottle of the château's white wine; and Yves turned courteously to the Saint to interpret the cryptic conversation.

'The Templars were believed to have amassed a tremendous fortune at the height of their prosperity. Louis Norbert has a theory that some of it could well have been stored in a Templar stronghold such as this.'

'If it had been, everyone would have been

looking for it when the castle fell,' Philippe said confidently. 'It is hardly likely that it would still be hidden after six hundred and forty years.'

'More likely the Templars took it with them,' Henri said.

'Perhaps they did not have the opportunity,' ventured Gaston.

'At any rate, it is an interesting dream,' said Yves, with soothing impartiality. 'And it harms nobody.'

The Saint was not so sure about that, but he said nothing.

In the space of a few minutes he had been presented with more information than he should have dared to hope for, but he did not propose to take sides in the debate. On the contrary, he had a sudden urge to efface himself as much as possible.

It was almost a relief when Mimette changed the subject by asking her father if he had heard the weather forecast for the next day, and Simon's rampant curiosity could take a breather while the conversation reverted to banalities.

The trout was followed by rare roast beef, pre-sliced in the kitchen and presented in the same style by Mrs Charles on a similar platter with its garniture of fresh vegetables. The Saint suppressed a pang at the reminder that French custom and cuisine, for all its artistry and refinement, would never admit that the best and only way to roast rare beef is on the rib, under its natural overcoat of self-basting fat, instead of trimming it down to a totally cholesterol-free dietician's boneless dream, dried on the outside and without richness within. The vegetables, however, were predictable perfection, a classic contrast to the Anglo-American school of stick-em-in-a-quart-of-water-and-boil-to-a-pulp. As an uninvited guest, it was up to him to enjoy the fare in the spirit in which it had been offered.

Mimette and Philippe appeared to have called a truce for the duration of the dinner. She talked with her father about the prospects for the harvest while her uncle became engrossed in a conversation with Henri about some new laws about labelling that were apparently about to come into force. Norbert spoke only when spoken to, which was not often.

Simon complimented Gaston on the red wine which Charles poured to accompany the beef, the same wine that had been recommended to him at lunch. From that it was an easy transition to the problems of a winery in wartime, and he found that once the old man's natural reserve was breached he made a fascinating companion. The Saint heard about his soldiering in the first war and his activities with the Resistance in the second. They were not the boasts of the dinner-table general but the mostly amusing, sometimes poignant, anecdotes of a private soldier. The more they talked the more the Saint warmed to him. But despite the soothing effects of the food and wine and his genuine interest in the stories, he also heard the conversations of the others around the table and was constantly alert for any additional background knowledge that he could pick up directly or indirectly.

Henri Pichot was apparently the local boy made good. His uncle Gaston had brought him up at Ingare; Philippe had spotted his potential and paid for him to study law in Paris. Having recently qualified he was now waiting to join a practice and in the meantime was working for one of Philippe's companies.

Philippe ran a number of companies and they made him a lot of money. He enjoyed talking about both, to the barely concealed boredom of Mimette.

After the meal came the formal adjournment to the salon, where Mrs Charles brought coffee and her husband served balloon glasses of brandy. Yves Florian took Simon by the arm and offered a cigar.

'If you don't mind, I'm trying to give up at least one vice every twenty years,' Simon declined. 'In that way I should achieve perfect purity by the time I'm a hundred.'

'I'm afraid I have been neglecting you. Mimette is always badgering me about the business. Even at meal times I get no peace.'

Yves looked across at his daughter and smiled fondly. There was clearly a very strong bond between them.

'Please don't feel guilty,' said the Saint. 'If I'm to stay for another day or two there will be plenty of time for us to talk.'

'I hope so. Because of the association with Ingare, your name has always caught my attention. I have followed your career, and I shall insist on boring you by asking you for the details that were not reported.'

'I should be delighted to tell you all, but if I do it may be me who turns out to be the bore.'

'I doubt it. I want particularly to hear about that affair of the Sons of France, ten years ago. You should have been given the Légion d'Honneur for that.'

The Saint laughed.

'I don't think it would have been politic at the time.'

'I suppose you are right,' Yves said sadly. 'There were too many powerful people involved. Fortunately most, if not all, came into the open during the occupation and have since been dealt with.'

As he spoke he seemed to glance towards Philippe. His words came through an unfortunate break in other conversations, and an uncomfortable stillness descended on the room.

It was Mimette who broke the silence. She made a play of looking at her watch and then stood up.

'Now Papa, this is no time to start

reminiscing about the war,' she said firmly. 'It's getting late, and as some of us have to make an early start in the morning I think we should make it an early night.'

Her father nodded, and the others who had been seated also rose.

'If you will excuse us,' he said, 'we have a long day ahead of us tomorrow.'

They walked out of the salon together.

'I could do with some fresh air,' Philippe announced. 'Come for a stroll in the garden, Henri. We can finish our discussion there.'

Pichot wished the Saint a good night. Philippe merely turned his back on the company and walked unsteadily into the garden.

Gaston and Norbert both bade the Saint their *bonnes nuits*, and Simon could think of nothing else to do but follow the example of the majority and wander back to his room.

He did not feel in the least tired, and his mind was too active to be ready for sleep. He took off his coat and tie but otherwise made no move to undress. He felt too restless even to lie on the bed, and slowly paced the room while he sorted over the clues that he had collected.

It was nearly eleven, but the night was still very warm. He opened the double doors and walked out on to the balcony. He surveyed the cloudless star-sprinkled sky for a long while and then lowered his gaze to roam over the valley. He followed the slope of the hill up to the château where the white of the castle walls stood out starkly against the blackness of the land. He thought again about the third man he had seen by the tower, and as he did so a faint light caught his eye. It was no bigger or brighter than the flare of a match and was just as quickly extinguished. It had appeared in one of the ground floor windows of the tower, and as he watched it burned again. This time it did not go out but moved slowly from side to side, creating a rhythmic pendulum of luminance. It looked like some kind of signal.

CHAPTER THREE

HOW HENRI PICHOT CONDUCTED AN EXPERIMENT, AND PROFESSOR NORBERT EXPLAINED A NAME

A half-moon added to the starlight of a cloudless sky revealed the garden and the walls clearly enough for the Saint's feline night vision. The light in the tower was stationary now, a faint flicker no more powerful than the glow of a candle but as bright as a beacon as far as he was concerned. It attracted him like a moth, and the thought of ignoring it never entered his head. His restlessness of a few minutes before was gone, submerged in the exhilarating prospect of direct action.

For a moment he considered returning to the dining-room and entering the garden that way, but he dismissed the idea almost immediately. It would be unwise to be found wandering through the château while his hosts and others slept, and there was also the risk of running into Philippe and Henri returning from their nocturnal stroll. But what would have been imprudent a few hours earlier was now a practical alternative.

The balcony on which he stood was directly above the one on the floor below, and he estimated that once he was hanging at full stretch he would have to drop no more than four or five feet to reach it. He would then be on a level with the top of the wall that ran from the château to the tower and the ten feet of brickwork separating the two was covered with a dense growth of ivy. The catwalk that had provided a beat for the castle's sentries was now only a couple of feet wide, but looked solid enough to serve his purpose.

The Saint went back into his room and took a dark blue pullover from his case to hide the whiteness of his shirt. He retrieved his throwing knife from beneath the pillow and strapped it on to his forearm as casually as another man might strap on a watch. He could perform tricks with that slender steel blade that would have guaranteed him a job in any circus, and he could draw and throw it faster than most men can produce a gun from a holster. He did not expect to have to demonstrate his skill that night but he believed in being prepared, and the gentle pressure of the leather sheath against his skin was quietly reassuring.

Back on the balcony he wasted no time reconsidering the course of action he had decided upon but swung a leg over the top of the balustrade and wedged his foot between two of the uprights. He repeated the manoeuvre so that he was balanced on the outside of the balcony facing towards the château and then carefully slid his hands down the supports until he was almost touching his toes. Calmly he stepped backwards into space with his fingers taking the strain of the deadweight of his body. Gently he began to rock his legs by kicking from the knees. With his face pressed against the deep base of the balcony he was unable to see the target he was aiming for and steadily increased the arc of his swing. As he swung in for the third time he released his hold. His momentum took him neatly over the edge, and he landed on his toes in the centre of the balcony below.

Fortunately the room it belonged to was in darkness, but he remained motionless in his crouch as he listened for any indication that he had been seen. Even when confident that he had not been observed, he kept below the height of the capstone until he reached the corner where it joined the château.

In the shadow of the wall he stood up and tugged at the ivy. The creepers had forced themselves deep between the bricks and only a few leaves came away. Satisfied that they would bear his weight, he stepped over the balustrade and reached out as far as he could to grasp one of the thick main stems of the vine.

His progress was quicker and easier than he had expected. The ivy was strong and well anchored, and its centuries of probing the mortar had opened up a score of fingerholds. Less than a minute after leaving the balcony the Saint dropped nimbly on to the catwalk and turned towards the tower. Bending low so as not to be silhouetted against the sky, he moved quickly along the wall until he reached the steps beside the tower. He took his time going down, taking the crumbling stairs one at a time and being careful not to dislodge the loose stones that littered them.

He sidled stealthily around the tower until he reached the window and just as cautiously ducked down and peered over the sill. When he had set out he had not bothered to speculate about what he might find, but the sight that greeted him was certainly stranger than any he would have imagined.

The tower was a hollow shell. The floors had long since collapsed, and the only clues to where they had once been were the positions of the arrowslits, the landings on the stone staircase that wound around the walls, and a single remaining joist that ran from just above the window to the opposite side of the room. From the centre, a slender stone pillar reached up halfway to the battlements.

The light that had caught his attention came from a small oil lamp hanging from the centre of the joist beside the pillar. Sitting around a table in its dim pool of light were Philippe, Henri, and Louis Norbert. In front of them lay a circle of cards bearing the letters of the alphabet, together with others on which had been scrawled the numbers from one to nine. The words '*oui*' and '*non*' had been written on two larger cards placed at opposite sides of the circle. An upturned wine glass was in the centre of the cards and the three men were staring intently at it as they rested the tips of their index fingers on its base.

The worldly Philippe Florian, the pedantic professor, and the diffident young lawyer were solemnly invoking the spirits . . .

With the sort of portentous gravity that politicians adopt when declaring war or raising taxes, Henri Pichot began to speak.

'Is anybody there?'

The Saint had to compress his lips to prevent the laughter escaping. He had always wondered what would happen at a séance if the medium's first question was answered in the negative.

The glass shivered and moved jerkily across the table to '*oui*' and then slid more smoothly back to the centre.

'Identify yourself,' Henri commanded, and the glass began to glide around the circle of cards, making a series of brief stops.

The professor read out the letters it visited: 'J.A.C.Q.U.E.S. D.E. M.O.L.A.Y.'

A sudden stillness descended on the group as the name registered. It lasted no more than a few seconds, but to the three men at the table it might as well have been an hour. They stared at the glass and even in the half-light the Saint could see Philippe stiffen and Norbert's eyes open wide in astonishment.

The movement of the glass back to the middle of the table broke the spell.

Philippe snatched his hand away as quickly as if the glass had become red hot, exclaiming: '*Mon Dieu!*'

Pichot looked nervously at the professor and his voice shook as he asked: 'Don't you think this has gone far enough?'

Norbert glared angrily at them.

'*Silence!*' he hissed. 'Do not break the circle. We are making a contact. There is nothing to be afraid of.'

Unconvinced but obviously unwilling to admit to fear, Philippe again laid his finger on the glass. Beads of sweat glistened on Norbert's temple, and he stared at the glass as if hypnotised.

The Saint turned away from the window towards the low door that led into the garden. It was half open and he moved silently towards it. As he did so he heard Norbert intone: 'When did you die?'

Cautiously the Saint peered in. The stone pillar stood between him and the three men, and the light of the oil lamp was too weak to spread beyond the table. Their whole attention was concentrated on the glass as the professor again read its answer out loud.

'1 . . . 3 . . . 1 . . . 4.'

The Saint slid through the narrow opening and sidestepped until he was directly in line with the pillar. He waited until the glass had returned to the centre of the table and the professor had asked for a message before moving. Three long swift strides brought him directly behind the pillar so that it completely hid him from the three men, but so close that he could have reached out and touched Henri's shoulder. The glass was moving again, faster this time, as if whoever or whatever controlled it was becoming more confident.

'T.H.O.S.E. W.H.O. H.A.V.E. T.H.E. C.O.U.R.A.G.E. T.O. S.E.E.K. S.H.A.L.L. W.I.N. T.H.E. R.E.W.A.R.D.S. O.F. T.H.E. B.R.A.V.E.' Norbert spelt out.

'What does it mean?' Philippe asked defiantly, but the professor again told him to be silent.

'Look, there is more,' said Henri.

The Saint edged round the pillar so that he could see what was happening.

The glass was sliding back and forth across the table, moving so rapidly that it was soon impossible to read out its message. First Philippe and then Norbert lost contact with it. Henri stayed with it for a few more seconds and then he too lost his touch. The glass was moving on its own. The colour drained from Philippe's face and Norbert was visibly shaking.

The glass shot towards Henri. The young man threw himself aside at the last moment as it flew off the table and shattered against the pillar an inch from the Saint's hand.

The Saint had never had cause to worry about the steadiness of his nerves, but the sight of the glass moving of its own accord and then seemingly heading straight at him had tested them to the full. He could not check the involuntary sideways movement that would have dodged a direct hit, any more than he could deny the eerie tingle he felt in the nape of his neck.

The three men jerked around as the glass splintered, and then he was sure enough of his self control to step calmly into the lamplight. He smiled broadly into their startled faces

'It didn't by any chance happen to mention the winner of tomorrow's big race at Chantilly?'

he enquired.

Gradually the others recovered from the shock caused by the flight of the glass and his own sudden materialisation. Philippe's chair crashed backwards as he stood up. He steadied himself with one hand against the table as he raised the other and pointed accusingly at the Saint.

'A trick! He's been making fools of us,' he shouted as the colour flooded back into his cheeks.

Simon's smile never wavered but his eyes were wary as he realised that Philippe was not only scared but also drunk, a combination that could be dangerous.

'Look, no hands,' he murmured, and raised his arms to emphasise the point.

Florian lurched towards him and there was no mistaking his intention. The Saint walked around the other side of the table to place its width between them. He had no wish to become involved in a brawl at this stage of the proceedings. Henri jumped up and placed a restraining hand on Philippe's shoulder.

'I think we should hear what Monsieur Templar has to say,' he said gently but firmly. Florian muttered something under his breath and leant back against the pillar glaring malevolently at the Saint.

Norbert still sat at the table. He looked up at the Saint and spoke as if questioning a student at

91

a tutorial.

'Well, Monsieur Templar? What are you doing here?'

'I came out for a breath of fresh air. I saw the light and wondered what was happening,' Simon replied easily. 'By the way, what *is* happening?'

'A scientific experiment,' the professor answered just as glibly.

'Funny, I thought you were prospecting.'

The Saint had not intended to say it. The words had simply formed themselves of their own accord and he had spoken them. Mimette's explanation for Norbert's late arrival at dinner and the amusement it caused, must, he decided, have been playing on his subconscious, which had duly produced an unexpected flash of insight.

Whatever its origin, his remark elicited an illuminating response. Philippe swore, and it was only Henri's grip on his shoulder that prevented him from trying to get close to the Saint again. For his part, Henri seemed suddenly very tense. But it was Norbert who provided the most surprising reaction. He simply smiled and rose slowly to his feet.

'So you are interested in the treasure?' he observed benignly.

Simon looked down into eyes as warm and welcoming as a pair of icebergs, and something he saw in their chill depths told him that the little professor was not just the comical gnome he appeared to be.

'Of course,' said the Saint guardedly.

'Why are you interested?' Florian snarled, but Norbert waved him to silence.

There was a new air of miniaturised authority about the professor which the Saint found fascinating.

'People have talked about the Templar treasure for hundreds of years, Monsieur Philippe. It is hardly a secret. The question is—how much does Monsieur Templar know?'

'Just what I've heard since I've been here,' the Saint answered adroitly, and before the point could be pressed he nodded towards the table and added: 'I take it you were asking for a little help from Heaven—or the other place.'

'I gather that you do not believe in such things,' said Norbert.

'Frankly, my tastes are more *spiritueux* than *spiritistes*.'

'I would have expected someone with your experience of the world to have a more open mind about such matters.'

The Saint heard the words but was no longer listening to them. He was looking past the three men towards the shadows beneath the far wall, and as he did so a strange chill rippled through him, as if his veins had turned into tiny rivers of ice.

From the gloom, a white shrouded figure was

watching them.

'We have a visitor,' Simon mentioned diffidently.

The professor had been rambling on about poltergeists, faith healing, and clairvoyance, as absorbed in propounding his own knowledge as only a man whose best friends are books can be. He was completely unaware that he had lost the attention of his audience until the Saint spoke. The others swung around. Henri gave a passable impression of someone trying to jump out of his skin, and almost tripped in his haste to place himself behind the table. Philippe was much calmer, or perhaps too befuddled to react sharply. He looked blearily from the Saint to the figure and waited on events. Norbert, taken completely aback, gawped at it with bulging eyes.

The Saint's own imperturbability was being put to a severe test. In the course of his eventful travels he had seen too much to be a total unbeliever, but for one quiet evening in Provence the spooky phenomena seemed to be coming somewhat thick and fast.

The figure began to move towards them. Slowly it emerged from the shade of the wall into one of the patches of moonlight that chequered the floor. The hazy white shrouded outline became focused into a flowing cotton cloak, and the apparition raised one hand and pulled back the cowl as it drew nearer. As they all saw the face, their relief might have seemed only a different kind of shock.

'A really spectacular entrance, Mademoiselle,' Simon congratulated her, with a slightly ironic bow.

The girl gave him a withering glance but appeared more concerned with the others. Her face was pale with rage and the knuckles of her clenched fists showed white. She stopped at the table and stood there with her hands on her hips inspecting each of them in turn, as a head mistress might have surveyed a group of truants.

Philippe was the first to recover.

'What do you mean by creeping up on us like that?' he blustered, stepping out to confront his niece. 'What are you doing here?'

Mimette rounded on him like a tigress.

'What am *I* doing here? This is my home! How dare you question me?'

'I hope we were not doing any harm,' Norbert put in placatingly. 'But you gave us all a start.'

'You deserved it,' Mimette retorted. 'I am surprised at you all. I thought you would have been above such childishness, Professor.'

'Our intention was far from childish, Mademoiselle,' Norbert countered. 'One should not make the mistake of thinking that because children do things they are necessarily childish.'

Mimette picked up a handful of the cards and threw them contemptuously back on to the table.

'Calling up the spirit of the glass? Most children forget such games before they are allowed to stay up so late.'

'A primitive method, I'll agree,' said Henri, as if conceding a minor point in a legal debate. 'But as we have no medium among us it had to serve our purpose.'

'Henri, I am disappointed in you,' Mimette replied. 'I would have thought you at least would have had more sense than to dabble in such rubbish.'

The young man avoided her eyes and seemed genuinely abashed.

'I'm sorry, Mimette. It was my silly idea. Just a little fun.'

The Saint rested his shoulders against the pillar completely at ease.

'I'm sorry if I broke any of the house rules,' he said, 'I couldn't get to sleep, and I was just wandering around—'

'You were not a party to it. I saw what happened. It was seeing you in the garden that brought me here.'

'Well, I am dreadfully sorry to have given offence, Mademoiselle Mimette,' Philippe declared aggressively, with as much dignity as he could muster.

With a parting scowl at his niece, he shouldered his way past Henri and Norbert and strode unsteadily out into the garden. Henri looked apologetically at Mimette.

'I think I'd better go and make sure he is all right,' he said, and hurried after him.

'Seeing that our experiment has been disrupted, I think I too shall retire,' the professor said pompously. As he passed Mimette he stopped and pointed to the crucifix hanging on a golden chain around her neck. 'Childish foolishness?' he sneered. 'I hope your talisman protects you.'

Grinning impishly, he ambled after the others.

'Alone again, at last,' Simon remarked when the professor had disappeared from view.

The girl was still quivering with suppressed rage, and for a moment he thought she was going to run after the professor and physically assault him. He moved over and put a restraining hand on her shoulder.

'It wouldn't be worth it,' he said, reading her mind.

Slowly she relaxed and he felt the tenseness drain away from her. She looked up at him with wide wondering eyes and seemed for a moment as vulnerable as a lost child.

'As if we didn't have enough to worry about,' she said at last, and there was a deep tiredness in her voice that revealed all the uncertainty behind her bold front of almost arrogant assurance.

'This place gives me the creeps—how about a

nightcap?' he suggested, and she nodded.

He reached up and unhooked the oil lamp, turning out the light as he placed it on the table. He kept his arm around her as they left the tower and strolled across the lawn to the dining-room.

She leant her head against his shoulder and whispered: 'Sometimes I wonder whether there really is a curse on us.'

He stroked her hair lightly.

'If you're cursed, I can think of millions of women who would be only too eager to line up at the witch's door.'

She met his eyes and smiled wickedly.

'Flattery will get you everywhere.'

'Flattery is only flattery when it isn't the truth,' he said.

In the drawing-room, while Mimette sank gratefully into the comfort of the sofa, he poured them both a long measure of Armagnac. He handed Mimette her glass and sat beside her.

'The professor keeps prattling on about his treasure. Do you believe in it?' he asked.

'It's a legend that must have some historic basis, I suppose. This was one of the last Templar strongholds to fall. The supposed wealth of the Templars was never fully accounted for. Perhaps it was exaggerated, but when the king's army finally broke in here they could find no trace of it. Those knights who were not killed escaped and were never captured.' Mimette laughed. 'It is said that the Devil took them down to hell.'

'But left the treasure up here—is that it?'

'Yes. People have searched for it for centuries but not even a single coin has been found. Even the Germans had a look for it. They were typically thorough and did a lot of damage but found nothing. How would you search a place as big as this, without a clue where to begin?'

'So why the sudden interest now?'

'Professor Norbert believes that the stone may be a clue to something, a sort of symbol map to where a treasure might be hidden.'

'Obviously he hasn't broken the code yet, or there would have been no need for the séance,' Simon observed.

Mimette's face darkened as she remembered the events in the tower.

'Norbert is obsessed with the treasure and I think he'd try anything to find it, even dabbling in the occult. And not only to prove his scholarship. I'm sure he'd also be delighted to make some money out of it.'

'And Philippe?'

'Uncle Philippe will try anything if there is likely to be a profit at the end,' she returned cynically. 'He's taken a great interest in Norbert's work. Sometimes I think that's why he wants to buy the château, just so that he can pull it down brick by brick to see if the treasure really is here. Then he could build a wine factory, nice and modern, nice and functional, and nice and profitable.'

'What did you mean about your father saving Philippe's life, and what was Yves's reference to the war all about?'

Mimette seemed to be considering the implications of answering as she gazed at the liquid in her glass.

At last she shrugged and said resignedly: 'What does it matter if you know? Philippe was in Paris during the war. He made a fortune on the black market.'

'Nothing so terrible in that,' said the Saint dispassionately. 'I suppose he had to make a living somehow.'

'No, not in itself,' Mimette agreed. 'But he was very friendly towards the Germans. People believed he was a collaborator and that that was why he was never arrested. He was more valuable giving the Germans information than he would have been in prison. There was a resistance group near Lille which Philippe had a connection with; I don't know all the details, but apparently he ran a sideline in forged identity papers, travel permits, that sort of thing. One night he was due to meet a contact. He never turned up but the Germans did. The whole group was rounded up and most of them were shot.'

'So why is he still around? I thought most collaborators didn't last long after the Allies arrived?'

'When Paris fell he came here, and Papa hid him for months. The word was put around that he had been killed in the street fighting before the city was liberated. It was easy to believe. People trusted my father, and anyway everything was in chaos. When things began to get back to normal and tempers had cooled, he returned to Paris. After all, the people he betrayed were dead, and there was no real proof against him. He used his money to open new businesses, and the richer he became the more powerful he was, and the harder it was to challenge him.'

'I know the type,' said the Saint drily. 'Endow a couple of charities, support the right political party, and suddenly you're a great guy and no one wants to remember.'

Mimette laughed shortly and without amusement.

'That's good old Uncle Philippe. The big dealer.'

'If all you've said is true, why does your father put up with him?'

'My father is a very gentle man. Although Philippe is only his half-brother—they had the same father but different mothers—he has always felt protective towards him. He believes it is all a question of family loyalties. He is blind to what Philippe is trying to do.'

'And you are not?'

Mimette rose and placed her empty glass on the table. She glanced at the clock and then at the Saint.

'It is very late, and we start the harvest as soon as it is light,' she replied with a return to the businesslike briskness that had so irritated him that afternoon. 'If you will excuse me, I am also very tired.'

He realised that nothing was to be gained by pressing her further and allowed his question to remain unanswered. He swallowed the last of his brandy and stood up.

'Until my car is repaired,' he said, 'if there's anything you'd like me to do—'

Mimette faced him inscrutably.

'Just keep your eyes open.'

At the door she turned.

'Could there by anything in supernatural explanations—in some destiny that forces some accidents to happen?'

'Such as?'

'After all,' she said, 'we seem to have been sent our very own Knight Templar to help us.'

The Saint gave her a courtly bow.

'*A vos ordres*,' he said.

She laughed again, and left him with a cheerful '*Dormez bien!*'

The sudden change of mood might have perplexed him if he had not witnessed a succession of similar transformations during the day. As it was, he accepted it as further evidence of what he was already afraid of. That Mimette Florian could be very close to a breakdown, and that her collapse might bring down the whole mysterious fabric of Château Ingare.

2

The Saint had never been convinced of the proverbial benefits ascribed to early rising. The nature of his vocation frequently entailed going to bed late and getting up at an hour when most of the population are contemplating lunch. So far as he could tell, the habit had done him little harm. It had certainly helped to make him wealthy, and appeared to have had no adverse effect on either his health or his wisdom. Furthermore, it had never developed in him any latent enthusiasm for catching worms.

Mimette had said that they started the harvest shortly after dawn but had considerately omitted to invite him to be present. Possibly she felt that he would only get in the way. In any case, he was grateful. He decided on a compromise between his normal inclination and the regime of the château, and opened his eyes as the grandfather clock on the landing outside his bedroom chimed for the ninth time.

He had slept the sound sleep that is supposed to be the prerogative of the innocent, and felt confident of being able to tackle anything the inhabitants of Château Ingare might throw in his way. He had not stayed awake considering

103

the implications of what Mimette had told him, being content to let the new day shed more light on the problems of the house. Nor did he allow them to worry him as he dressed but concerned himself solely with the selection of the day's wardrobe.

He met Charles in the corridor outside his room, and the old man informed him that he had been just about to wake him.

'Clairvoyance is another of my gifts,' said the Saint breezily. 'And where do I break my fast?'

'The dining-room, m'sieu,' Charles replied and added that his hosts and fellow guests had already eaten. 'Is there anything special you would like?'

'Could you manage ham and eggs?'

'Of course.'

Simon followed him down to the reception area. The double doors of the old hall were open and the Saint stopped and looked in. The muffled sounds of hammering reached him.

'A woodpecker must have got in,' he observed, and the servant allowed himself a half-smile.

'I understand Professor Norbert is doing some restoration in the chapel.'

'Sounds more as if he's trying to dig his way out,' Simon commented, as Charles ushered him into the dining-room.

One of the hardships of travelling in the country of *haute cuisine* is that the French have never discovered the delicious potential of real bacon or the proper art of frying eggs. However, the ham and eggs which he had ordered, cooked together in the inevitable little porcelain dish, would provide the solid sustenance which Simon Templar deemed an essential start to the day, in addition to a freshly baked *croissant* and some home-made jam. After disposing of them, he poured a second cup of coffee and picked up the copy of the newspaper that had been left beside his place.

He scanned the pages but found little of interest. The French government was in danger of falling, which in those days was as regular as rain in April, and there was speculation about a general strike. These and a stepping up of the war in Indo-China were allocated about half the space devoted to the fact that a lady in Toulouse had produced sextuplets. As he turned to an even more exhaustive coverage of a rumoured romance between a royal prince and a nude dancer at the *Folies Bergère*, Charles entered to inform him that the mechanic from the local garage had arrived.

Simon's first view of the said mechanic was the soles of a pair of very large boots protruding from under the front of the Hirondel. He wished them good morning and was rewarded with the appearance of a pair of grease-stained hands that curled out and gripped the bumper. Gradually the rest of the mechanic hauled himself into view.

'What a beautiful car, monsieur,' the man enthused. 'Such an engine! Such workmanship! Such elegance!'

'I'm glad you approve,' said the Saint. 'Can you fix it?'

The mechanic shook his head.

'No. It will need a new radiator.'

'Can you get a new radiator?'

The mechanic considered the question carefully as if the idea had not occurred to him before. Finally he nodded.

'There is a dealer in Nice. I will send for one straight away and have it delivered express,' he replied, plainly looking forward to the prospect of closer contact with the car's intestines.

'How long will that take?'

'With luck I could get one here by midday tomorrow.'

The Saint looked around to make quite sure that there was no one within earshot, before he peeled a couple of notes from his wad and pressed them into the hands of the startled mechanic.

'Why not run out of luck until Friday?' he suggested.

'But that is several days, monsieur,' the man exclaimed.

Simon added a third note to the man's collection.

'So it is,' he agreed as the argument

disappeared into the mechanic's pocket. 'Look, I'm in no great hurry so why don't you get the radiator delivered and wait till I call and ask how much longer the job will take?'

'But monsieur... ?' the man began; but the Saint clapped him on the shoulder and propelled him gently towards the breakdown truck that had brought him.

'Just give me the name of your garage and be on your way.'

He took the greasy card that the mechanic offered, and watched while the Hirondel was hitched up to the tow crane. A fourth and conclusive sample of the Banque de France's elegant artwork found its way into the mechanic's possession as he climbed into his truck.

'This is of course strictly between ourselves,' Simon whispered conspiratorially.

'Of course, monsieur,' the man agreed, and drove quickly away in case the mad foreigner should change his mind and demand his money back.

The Saint smiled to himself at the ease with which the problem of extending his stay had been overcome. He hoped that the unknown saboteur, whoever it was, would appreciate his co-operation.

He strolled back into the château and again stopped to listen to the noise of Norbert's industry. The violent pounding he had first heard had changed to a rhythmic tap-tap-tap of metal on stone. As he stood deciding whether or not to interrupt the professor's labours he heard the door of the salon open.

He turned expecting to see Charles or his wife, but instead found himself looking at a girl who might have walked straight out of the pages of a movie magazine.

She was a platinum blonde with the sort of figure that makes an hour-glass look tubular. She wore a silky white dress that was long at the hem and low at the top and tight in-between. She had the long-lashed bedroom eyes and full red lips that are more usually seen smiling out of glossy magazines in the cause of selling anything from deodorants to dog food. It was standardised beauty which the Saint could appreciate without being swept off his feet. She was not so much standing in the doorway as posing there, with one hand resting lightly on her hip and the other holding an unlit cigarette an inch from her lips.

Her voice held exactly the right note of practised allure he would have expected.

'Do you have a light?'

'I'm afraid not. They told me that smoking would stunt my growth.'

The girl eyed him shamelessly and smiled.

'You seem big enough already.'

'I lead a very pure life,' he informed her solemnly. 'They also told me never to speak to strange ladies until we'd been introduced.'

The girl turned away and walked back into the salon. The Saint followed, picked up the table lighter and lit her cigarette without bothering to ask why she had been unable to perform the task for herself.

'Thanks. I am Jeanne Corday.'

'Simon Templar. *Et enchanté*.'

'The Saint!'

In her surprise the girl's accent slipped from Parisian *pointu* to the twang of Marseille. Simon noticed the lapse but it was quickly corrected.

'The famous Simon Templar! What brings you to a mortuary like this? No one's been murdered, have they?'

'Not yet, to my knowledge, but you never know your luck,' he said. 'And you? I wouldn't say this was your natural *ambience*.'

'I'm here for the harvest.'

'Picking or grape-treading?' he asked politely. She laughed.

'Hardly. I'm here to be presented to the powers that be for approval. I'm Henri Pichot's fiancée.'

The Saint blinked in surprise. Philippe's mistress he could have believed. A school friend of Mimette's, lured away by bright lights, even. But the prospective spouse of the timid lawyer? It seemed a laughable combination.

'Well, well, well. Happy Henri,' he said thoughtfully.

Jeanne Corday interpreted it as a compliment, and smiled to display a set of expensively white teeth.

'Have you just arrived?' he asked, mainly because he could think of little else to say.

'This morning. I came down on the sleeper from Paris. Henri collected me from Avignon and here I am.'

'Where is the lucky man?'

She sighed with affected boredom. 'Off playing the peasant somewhere, I suppose, and leaving me all alone to amuse myself. What does one do all day in a place like this?'

'I'm not sure,' the Saint admitted. 'But I'm going to go and join the peasants. Fancy a walk? It's only a kilometre or so to the battlefields.'

'Walk!' the girl grimaced in disgust. 'Do you mind?'

'Not in the least. See you later, then.'

She scowled as if he had insulted her. She was obviously unaccustomed to being rejected so easily but said nothing as he left her.

The Saint sauntered leisurely out of the château grounds following the track he had been driven along the previous day. It was a beautiful morning with a light breeze tempering the heat of the sun. The fields bordering the path were full of workers picking the grapes and piling them into huge wicker baskets. The air hummed with their chatter and the rattle of the handcarts as they were trundled up the hill towards the cluster of buildings below the château. Everything around him seemed light-years away from long dead knights, family curses, saboteurs and séances, and it was an effort to think about such things.

But the idea of hidden treasure intrigued him. Certainly it seemed to provide the basis of a motive for Philippe's interest in buying the château and even for trying to ruin the business so that Yves Florian would be forced into selling. But he was also a successful businessman and such men do not become rich by chasing legends. Norbert's position was easier to understand. The professor was concerned with the historic importance of the treasure as well as its possible financial value. The kudos he could earn as its finder would be as sweet as any material reward he might claim. Only Henri's rôle was vague, and the arrival of his fiancée made it even cloudier. To attract such a woman he must have more to offer than the average undistinguished lawyer.

The Saint was so absorbed in his thoughts as he climbed the second hill towards the barn that he did not immediately recognise an approaching figure, but as they drew closer he waved a greeting and the other stopped and waited for him.

'*Bonjour*, Gaston,' Simon said heartily. 'I'm afraid I'm not very early. Is Mimette around?'

'Yes, she is at the barn. Is your car repaired

yet?'

'No. It needs a new radiator, and the mechanic says he won't be able to get hold of one for some days,' the Saint replied, glibly combining fact and fiction.

His answer seemed to distress the old man. Gaston shuffled his feet nervously and looked back up the path as if he was afraid of being followed.

'What is the matter?' Simon asked.

For a while the foreman said nothing but simply stared searchingly at the Saint. When he finally spoke there was no mistaking the earnestness behind his words.

'Do not wait for your car, Monsieur Templar. Go now. Go while you still can.'

'What is that supposed to mean?' Simon demanded.

'I cannot explain but I hope you will listen,' Gaston pleaded. 'Go now, or you may not leave Ingare alive.'

3

At any other time such a melodramatic prognostication might have made the Saint laugh, but he did not even smile as he realised the change that had come over Gaston Pichot in the twelve hours since they had chatted so casually together at dinner. Then the old overseer had been eager to begin the harvest and his greatest worry had been the quality and quantity of the coming vintage. Now he seemed bowed by cares he was not used to bearing and he was afraid. It was the fear in the old man's eyes which the Saint found so hard to understand and which made him appreciate the seriousness of the warning. The Saint's arrival had often depended on his ability to judge a man's character on the briefest of encounters and he knew that Gaston Pichot was not usually given to displays of dramatics or of fear. Men who jump at shadows do not survive five years in the Resistance.

Gaston seemed to read the answer to his advice in the Saint's face. He sighed deeply and shook his head.

'But you will not leave,' he stated flatly. 'I knew that you wouldn't, but it was my duty to warn, perhaps, an old comrade.'

He started to walk away but the Saint stopped him.

'Warn me of what, Gaston? Who is going to do me in?'

'Would it make any difference if I told you?'

The Saint smiled.

'Probably not, but it might save me from coming to an untimely end.'

Gaston waved a hand towards the slopes where the grapes were being gathered.

'The men have heard what happened at the séance last night. I don't know how. I did not know about it myself until one of them told me.

113

It was a foolish thing to do. They are very superstitious and the tale has grown with the telling. They are saying that the Templar curse is coming true and that your arrival is linked with it. The burning of the barn has worried them. If anything else happens I am afraid of what they might do.'

Despite the other's obvious sincerity, the Saint found it hard to take that threat seriously.

'What are you suggesting? A lynch mob?'

'With a mob, you never know,' Gaston replied gravely. 'But I do not think it is only them you have to fear.'

'Who, then?' Simon persisted. 'Philippe?'

Gaston shook off his detaining hand.

'I have said enough already. Perhaps too much. I could be wrong.'

Again he began to walk away, and this time the Saint did not try to stop him. He knew instinctively that however hard he pressed his questions he would find out nothing more. He stood and watched the overseer trudge stolidly up the hill towards the château before he continued his own journey.

He played back the conversation in his mind as he walked, analysing every word and gesture in an attempt to understand what could have prompted Gaston's action. He only half believed the story of unrest among labourers in the vineyard. Superstitious they might be, but he doubted that their fears would be translated into any action that could endanger him. If Gaston had used their threat as a blind then there was only one plausible alternative: that he was trying to protect someone else, not from what they had done but from what they might do.

The smoke-blackened ruin of the barn was the centre of activity. The inside had been cleared, and the debris of the fire piled against the walls. Mimette stood beside the truck, supervising its loading as the labourers humped their baskets of grapes from the surrounding fields and emptied them into the rows of bins lined up by the tailboard.

'How's it going?' Simon asked cheerily.

'Very well,' she replied, wiping her forehead with the sleeve of her blouse. 'It should be a bumper crop this year. God knows we need one.'

He slipped of his jacket and began rolling up his sleeves.

'Where shall I start?'

'Start?' Mimette repeated blankly.

'Yes, start. You know—begin, commence, proceed, get down to it, etcetera.'

'You mean you want to help with the harvest?'

'But of course,' he said indignantly. 'If I can't sing for my supper I'll pick for it.'

'You're not exactly dressed for work,' she protested, and he admitted to himself that most vineyard workers do not clock on wearing silk

115

shirts and Savile Row trousers.

He lowered his voice confidentially.

'My tailors would have coronaries, but if you don't tell them I won't.'

Mimette handed him a basket. She led him to a row of vines and briefly instructed him in the correct method of clipping the bunches.

'And if I see you slacking I'll dock your pay,' she told him sternly.

The Saint tugged his forelock.

'*Oui, mademoiselle*,' he said humbly, in a creditable imitation of the local accent.

She laughed as she left him to his work. He had had no intention of lending a hand when he left the château. The idea had been spontaneous. He believed in collecting experiences. He had never taken part in a grape harvest. Here was a grape harvest, so why not take part?

He discovered that grape-picking was far harder work than it appeared and it tested even his stamina. After two hours of non-stop toil in the heat of the day he had managed to locate muscles he had forgotten existed, and his hands and arms were stained a dark purple from the juice that burst from the ripe fruit.

He talked to the other pickers as he carried his basket to and from the truck. Including Pascal and Jules, they were respectful and distant—and, he guessed, suspicious of his working among them. But there was no sign of the hostility that Gaston had tried to hint at.

A halt was called at midday and he sat beside Mimette in the shade of the cypress trees, tucking in to coarse bread, *saucisson*, strong cheese and *vin* very *ordinaire* with the same relish as if it had been a meal at Maxim's. When both hunger and thirst had been sated he told her of his encounter with Jeanne Corday.

'I heard that she arrived this morning,' she said. 'What is she like?'

He considered his reply carefully.

'Can you imagine a cross between Mae West, Marlene Dietrich, and a playful boa constrictor?' he enquired.

Mimette's eyes widened incredulously.

'She can't be such a mixture as that!'

'That's just my impression, and don't quote me. Where did Henri meet her?'

'In Paris, I suppose. The first I heard about it was when he wrote to Gaston saying he had become engaged.'

'I think poor old Gaston is in for a surprise,' Simon chuckled. 'By the way, where is Henri?'

'I'm not sure. I think he said he was going to check the inventory at the *chai*.'

'And Philippe?'

Mimette scowled.

'Uncle Philippe does not believe in soiling his hands. He went into Avignon early this morning, saying he had business to attend to. I don't care where he is as long as he keeps out of my way.'

'Well, you should,' he told her reprovingly. 'First rule of warfare, always know the enemy's position.'

'Then you do believe Philippe is the enemy,' she said, but the Saint refused to be drawn.

'Let's just say he is a prime suspect, and leave it at that for the time being.'

He stood up. The other workers were returning to the fields but he made no move to join them. The truck was full and about to begin another trip to the *chai*.

'It's been fun, but I think I'd better get back to some real work,' he told Mimette as he helped her up.

'Real work?'

'You remember, keeping your eyes open. I'll hitch a lift back to base and see what's happening. I'd like to take the professor up on his offer of a chat.'

'You're sure it's the professor you want to see and not Jeanne Corday?' Mimette enquired mischievously.

The Saint appeared suitably shocked.

'How could you suspect such a thing?' he asked in a tone of injured innocence.

As they walked towards the truck he said casually: 'By the way, the *garagiste* came, and says he can't repair your handiwork for some days.'

The girl's cheeks flushed, and she looked

down at her shoes to avoid his eyes.

'How did you know it was me?'

'Elementary, my dear Mimette,' Simon answered in his best Holmesian voice. 'Whoever damaged the car wanted me to stay, and you were the only person who didn't seem anxious to get rid of me. Anyway, I've a feeling that filing down the brake cables would have been more to a villain's taste.'

'I'm sorry, but I had to go out and it was the only thing I could think of at the time,' said Mimette shamefacedly. 'However long it takes, you must stay with us.'

'I'll be delighted to. And I'll keep the secret. Just one thing . . .'

'Yes?' she asked quickly, and the Saint smiled.

'Next time try cutting the radiator hose. It doesn't make half as much mess.'

For a moment she was nonplussed and then she began to giggle like a schoolgirl caught playing a prank.

The memory of her high-spirited merriment stayed with him during the bumpy ride back to the château. She was a different person from the confused and angry woman he talked with the previous night, more at home in the fresh air and freedom of the fields than the heavy cloistered atmosphere of the château; and he had deliberately kept the conversation light to try and take her mind off her problems.

The driver dropped him at the château steps before taking his load around to the *chai*. He saw no sign of Jeanne Corday as he walked across the reception area and through the old hall to the chapel. Louis Norbert was on his hands and knees in the centre of the aisle, using a wire brush to scrub away the dirt that had filled in the letters of a tombstone set into the floor. He glanced up as the Saint entered.

'Yes?' he enquired curtly, with no attempt to conceal his irritation at being disturbed.

'Or no, as the case may be,' the Saint responded blandly.

'Do you want something?'

'A word. Several, in fact,' said the Saint as he perched on top of a pew directly in front of the professor, so that his shadow obscured the tombstone. 'I thought I'd take you up on your invitation to discuss my pedigree.'

'I thought you refused to be serious about that,' said Norbert crossly, but the Saint only smiled.

'I was too hasty,' he conceded. 'The past twenty-four hours have made me very interested in the Templars.'

'And their treasure, no doubt,' the professor amplified slyly.

'And their treasure,' Simon agreed. 'But then I suppose it really is just a legend.'

The little man sniggered. It was a high-pitched cackle that was strangely sinister. He

120

straightened up and peered fixedly at his visitor.

'A legend? Perhaps. Troy was only a legend until Schliemann dug it up. Tutankhamun was thought an insignificant pharaoh before Carter opened the tomb,' he snorted. 'What is a legend but a memory distorted by time? The treasure of the Templars exists and I shall find it.'

'I hope so,' said the Saint pleasantly, and Norbert rounded on him.

'You hope so! Why? So you can steal it? You are like the others. You think only of money. You think only in terms of gold and silver and jewels.'

'And you think in terms of acclaim from your academic cronies,' countered the Saint calmly. 'Name in the newspapers, radio interviews, and a bestselling book: *How I Found The Lost Treasure*. Right? So now we understand each other there is no need to quarrel. But what was that mumbo-jumbo about in the tower last night?'

'One of the charges against the Templars was that they practised black magic. You may scoff at the occult but—'

'I know, I know,' interrupted the Saint wearily. 'More things in heaven and earth, and so on and so forth. Okay, so let's suppose you made contact with something or someone last night. Who was this Jacques de Molay you were all so excited about?'

Norbert regarded him coldly.

'Your arrogance is surpassed only by your ignorance.'

The Saint let the insult pass. He had a feeling that Norbert was the brand of academic who could not resist giving a lecture at the drop of a question, and he was right. The little man paced up and down the aisle as he talked.

'Jacques de Molay was the last Grand Master of the Order of the Templars. After King Philip he was the most important man in France. One of the most important in all Europe. Philip lured him and the other leading Templars into a trap. He invited them to Paris, pretended to befriend them, and when they were all gathered in the Temple he had them arrested. Simultaneously his men swooped on all the major Templar strongholds.'

'Including Ingare?'

'Of course. The knights resisted, but de Molay let them down. Under torture he admitted all the crimes he was accused of—heresy, betrayal of the Crusades, treason to the Pope, everything. After that the knights lost heart.'

'I wouldn't be too hard on him, Professor,' said the Saint gently. 'How would you feel if someone was offering to make you two metres tall in a few easy stretches?'

'But with his confession the Pope was forced to act,' said Norbert implacably. 'He endorsed Philip's actions and the Templars were officially proscribed. If de Molay had remained firm, they might have survived.'

'According to your séance, he died in 1314. But according to a student I met on the road yesterday that was years after the Templars were disbanded. What happened in between?'

'The Templars were put on trial. It was all a sham, of course. De Molay was burnt at the stake. As he died, he summoned both the king and the Pope to meet him before the throne of judgement within a year. Both died within a few months. Something for even a sceptic like you to think over,' Norbert gibed.

'Impressive enough,' Simon assented. 'De Molay would, of course, have known all about the treasure.'

'Of course. It was probably he who arranged for some of it to be brought to Ingare. Not that the fortress was known by that name then. The word was found carved into the stone in the great hall, and the new owners adopted it. For centuries it has been the only clue to the location of the treasure.'

'What does it mean?'

'It is an anagram of *Regina*,' Norbert said, as if only an idiot would have failed to recognise it.

The Saint frowned.

'The Latin word for Queen? Queen of what?'

'I do not know. If I did, I might have already found the treasure. Last night we might have been told, but you ruined it.'

123

'It was hardly my fault,' the Saint pointed out mildly. 'Your spook seemed to take an instant dislike to me.'

The professor stopped his pacing. He stood glaring venomously at the Saint and shaking with anger.

'You were meddling in matters that did not concern you, and you are meddling again now.' Norbert's voice rose to a shriek. 'Get out! Go away. Leave me to my work. Leave me in peace!'

The Saint looked steadily into a pair of eyes that seemed to glow with a secret fire, and for the first time he wondered whether Professor Louis Norbert was completely sane. He could think of little that might be gained by staying, and turned compliantly away. By the time he reached the door Norbert was back on his knees, frantically scrubbing at the marks on the floor.

The Saint strolled out into the fresh air of the garden and sat on the edge of the wall. Except for some interesting historical background he had learnt little. He was wondering what to do next when the decision was made for him.

A scream and a crash of falling masonry drifted up from the direction of the *chai* and outbuildings below the château, and he was on his feet and racing towards them before the echo had died.

He covered the first hundred metres in a

fraction over eleven seconds and reached the entrance to the nearest storehouse at the same time as the men who had been unloading the truck outside.

In the centre of the flagstone floor was a jagged hole, and lying ten feet down, half buried beneath broken wood and shattered paving, was the spreadeagled body of Gaston Pichot.

CHAPTER FOUR

HOW GASTON MADE
A DISCOVERY, AND
PHILIPPE FLORIAN
TOOK CHARGE

As he looked down at the sprawled figure Simon experienced a disorientating isolation from the surrounding confusion. The excited shouts of the labourers and the thud of their heavy boots on the flagstones drifted into a remote background. He was totally aware of everything that had happened yet was apart from it. He stood motionless, numbed by an eerie feeling of *déjà vu*, as if the events of the preceding seconds were no more than stills from a film he had seen before.

With cool detachment he searched for a reason and found it in the veiled warning that

Gaston had delivered a little earlier. The old man's words returned to jar him back to reality.

'*Accidents happen.*'

In the instant of his return to his usual alertness Simon realised three things. The first was that Gaston was not fatally injured, for he was already clambering to his knees. The second was that the workmen were turning to him as if for an explanation. And the third was a vibration he could feel beneath his feet.

'Back!'

The urgency in his voice made the others jump to obey even before they appreciated the danger. No sooner had they retreated from the edge than another section of the floor collapsed on the opposite side of the hole from where the Saint stood.

A string of oaths rose with the cloud of dust that followed the cave-in, and the Saint grinned with relief in the assurance that no one capable of such a voluble and coherent attack on the parentage and peculiarities of his would-be rescuers could yet be written off. He knelt down, carefully spreading his weight more evenly, and peered into the gloom below. Gaston was on his feet, brushing the dust and dirt from his clothes and hair with one hand as he massaged the small of his back with the other.

'Are you all right?'

Gaston looked up, clearly surprised to hear

the Saint's voice, and winced at the pain the sudden movement caused him.

'I think so, monsieur,' he replied hesitantly. 'At least there are no bones broken.'

'What happened?'

'I was rolling a barrel across the floor when it just gave way. You had best be careful, the supports down here are all rotten. I cannot imagine how they have lasted so long.'

'That's what they said to Methuselah,' Simon rejoined. 'We'll have you out in a minute. Stay in the centre in case any more of the floor collapses.'

He moved cautiously back from the edge and turned to speak crisply to the men nearest to him.

'You, get some rope and a ladder. You get a flashlight. You go to the château, tell anyone you find there what has happened and bring back a first aid box. The rest of you stay outside, we don't want any more accidents.'

The workmen hurried to carry out his instructions. Simon perched himself on one of the barrels stacked by the door and waited for them to return.

Had it not been for Gaston's prophetic warning he would have found nothing very extraordinary in what had happened. He recalled his visit to the chapel the previous day, and Gaston's accident merely confirmed what he had surmised then, that the hill beneath the château was likely to be a warren of cellars and tunnels dating back to the building of the original fortress. Like the rest of the house they would have been extended piecemeal as required with little concern as to how long they would have to last. In such circumstances, subsidences were bound to be occasional events. It would have been satisfying to have found a more sinister explanation for what had happened, but it was evident that Gaston had been alone in the storehouse and the odds against the accident having been engineered were too long to be taken seriously.

The sounds that reached him indicated that Gaston Pichot had no intention of keeping still until he was rescued, and Simon had just decided to find out what he was doing when the labourers began to return.

The Saint tied an end of the rope to one of the two powerful flashlights they had brought and then laid the ladder on the floor and slid it towards the hole. Treading as lightly as possible on the rungs, he carried the rope and the flashlights to the hole.

Gaston was on his hands and knees in the gloom and appeared to be sifting through the debris when the Saint found him with the beam of the second torch.

'I'm lowering a light so that you can see where to guide the ladder,' Simon told him as he began to pay out the rope.

Once he had a clear view of the bottom of the hole, Simon tipped the ladder over the edge, positioning it as near vertically as possible to lessen the strain on the floor. As soon as it was in place he shinned nimbly down with the other lamp.

'There is no need, I can manage,' said Gaston huffily, but Simon ignored him.

Now that he was sure that the overseer was not gravely hurt he was impatient to find out what lay below. Gaston held his light on the bottom of the ladder until the Saint reached it, and then raised the beam to illuminate the room they stood in.

The combined brilliance of their two lamps showed it in detail. It was about twenty feet square and nine feet high. The walls and what was left of the ceiling were made of trimly hewn stone blocks, while the floor consisted only of the smoothed rock of the hill. Jutting from three of the walls seat-high from the ground were boxed-in stone benches that reminded Simon of the tombs of monks he had seen in abbeys, although the general appearance suggested an ante-room rather than a burial chamber.

He took in the layout of the room with one sweeping glance until his gaze reached the far wall.

On a low intricately carved plinth stood one of the strangest statues he had ever seen.

It was a life-sized marble sculpture of a

woman dressed in a flowing Grecian-style costume. Pawing at her dress like lap dogs were a pair of baying wolves which she was affectionately stroking. The Saint had an involuntary shudder as he took in the head. There was no sign of the classical beauty he had half expected: instead, the sculptor had fashioned not one face but three, each as hideous as the other. The mouths were fixed in tight-lipped snarls that copied the menace of the wolves, and the noses were hooked like scythes. The eyes held no expression at all. They were simply deep black voids. Framing the features was a wild mass of tangled hair that tumbled down the figure's back and over her breasts like a nest of angry snakes. Between her feet stood a small iron-bound oak casket which seemed to contain a few tiny scraps of brittle yellow parchment.

'Must have been somebody's dream girl,' the Saint remarked, and was surprised to find himself whispering like a tourist in a cathedral.

He walked around the rubble in the middle of the floor and approached the statue, conscious that wherever he moved the sightless eyes seemed to follow him.

Gaston stayed where he was.

'It is evil, monsieur,' he declared.

The old man was both excited and afraid. He shuffled his feet nervously and glanced anxiously at the ladder as he waited for the

Saint.

Simon picked up the casket and inspected it. The wood was splintered where the lid had been levered open and there were bright scratches on the edges of the lock. It carried no clue to its original owner and was too small to contain a hidden compartment. The pieces of parchment were brittle to the touch and blank except for a few faded strokes that might have been the tops of letters. Regretfully he replaced it on the ledge and turned to face Gaston.

'Too bad it's empty,' he said.

'Yes, yes it is,' Pichot agreed restlessly. 'A great pity.'

Simon promptly turned back to the ladder.

'I'm sorry, Gaston. I was forgetting that you must still be very shaken.'

'I have strained my back,' the other said with a grimace. 'But it could have been much worse.'

'Can you climb?'

'I think so.'

'I'll hold the ladder for you. Take your time.'

The old man began to pull himself up rung by rung. Simon waited until he was at the top and then followed. One of the labourers helped his foreman to safety, and as Gaston sat on a cask to regain his breath the workman Simon had sent to the château returned accompanied by Henri and Norbert.

Briefly Gaston told them what had happened. Henri took a small bottle from his pocket and his uncle gratefully sampled its contents.

'It was very fortunate that you were here, Monsieur Templar,' Henri said stiffly. 'It seems that once again we are in your debt.'

'I do seem to have a habit of being around when things happen, don't I?' said the Saint. 'But I didn't really do anything.' He directed Henri back to Gaston, who was again on his feet. 'Don't you think you had better see him home?'

'Of course,' Henri agreed. 'Come, uncle. I have a car outside, and the doctor has been sent for.'

'There is no need for so much fuss,' Gaston grumbled; but he allowed Henri to take his arm and lead him out. Norbert did not follow. He was trying to peer into the hole in the floor, hopping about like an excited bird.

'A hidden chamber—this is really exciting!'

'I thought that's what you'd be most concerned about,' Simon said drily. 'Here, take a flashlight and go and have a look.'

Even though the Saint had become accustomed to Norbert's excitable nature the intensity of his reaction when he finally managed to negotiate the descent and saw the statue for the first time was quite a spectacle. The professor gawped at the figure, his face a study of joyous amazement like a child unexpectedly presented with a long coveted toy.

'Incredible! Quite incredible,' he breathed,

and almost tripped over in his hurry to get a closer look.

Simon had followed more coolly, and was content to give the professor his head until his examination was completed and his excitement had subsided sufficiently to allow him to answer questions.

Louis Norbert ran his hands over the grotesque figure as gently as if it were made of the finest bone china. He got down on his knees and minutely traced the carving on the plinth. Simon took in the details of the column for the first time and saw that they depicted a tree through whose heavy foliage peered the contorted faces of what were presumably meant to be wood spirits and devils.

Norbert minutely studied each of the wolves in turn before running his hands up the folds of the dress until by stretching on tiptoe he could glide his fingers over the features of the face. All the while the examination was in progress a steady flow of mumbled superlatives told Simon how important the professor believed the statue to be.

'Well?' Simon prompted at last, when both Norbert's examination and supply of adjectives appeared to be temporarily exhausted.

The professor turned sharply, irritated at having his thoughts disturbed.

'What?'

'That kind of dialogue will get us nowhere,'

Simon rebuked him with a smile. However hard he tried he found it difficult to take the academic's antics seriously. 'What is it?'

'Hecate,' Norbert replied, as if exasperated by such basic ignorance.

Simon searched back through the mythology he had picked up in serependipitous reading. Except for the amorous exploits of Zeus and a feeling of kinship with Odysseus and Jason, he admitted that he had never been deeply drawn into the subject.

'Greek goddess?' he hazarded, hoping that it would act as a cue for one of the professor's instant lectures.

He was not disappointed. Norbert backtracked until he stood by the Saint's side but his eyes continued to absorb every detail of the statue as he spoke.

'Originally, yes. A minor deity. Not one of the true Olympians.'

'Poor girl,' said the Saint.

The professor ignored him.

'She was the goddess of ghosts and the creatures of the night. The queen of graveyards and of the spirits of the lost. Later she became the ruler of witches and all who followed the paths of darkness. A hymn to Hecate was part of the necromancer's ritual.'

'Sounds like a dead end job,' Simon remarked, but before Norbert could take offence he added: 'Why the three faces and the wolves?'

'Wolves were seen as creatures of evil in the Middle Ages. As for the three faces, they represent the triplicity of her nature. She is powerful in heaven, on earth, and in hell. Also she embodies the stages of the moon, waxing, full and waning. She was believed to haunt crossroads and it was at crossroads that witches were buried,' Norbert explained.

'What do you make of this place?' Simon asked, and for the first time the professor bothered to look away from the statue and consider the rest of the chamber.

'Obviously a part of the original fortress. I would surmise that it might once have been a meeting place.'

'So the knights would have been responsible for the statue. And hence the anagram of *Regina*. But I thought they were supposed to be militant Catholics.'

'You do not listen,' Norbert said testily. 'I told you that one of the charges made against the Templars was that they practised black magic. Generally it was most certainly a lie; but here, perhaps, it may have been true.'

'Doesn't anything strike you as odd about this room?' Simon asked, and after a brief glance around Norbert shook his head.

'No. What is wrong?'

'Well,' Simon pointed out, 'we are here because the floor of the storehouse and the roof

135

of this chamber collapsed. If you look up, you'll see that there is the ceiling of this room, then a layer of rock, above which is a few centimetres of soil, and then there are the flagstones which are the floor of the storehouse.'

'So what?'

'So how did anyone get in here in the old days?'

Norbert looked from the Saint to the ceiling, and then turned his flashlight over every wall and corner.

'There is no door!' he exclaimed, when he had finally authenticated the statement.

'For a great scholar, you do catch on fast,' said the Saint mockingly.

The professor glowered, and Simon patted him consolingly on the head.

'Never mind—we can't all go to the same schools. But now we had better get out of here in case any more of the ceiling falls in.'

'But you don't realise how important this is! I have work to do,' Norbert protested.

'And you are not going to be able to do it if half a ton of rock lands on your head. You can come back when it's been shored up.'

The authority in the Saint's voice brooked no argument and with a last longing look at the statue Norbert began to climb up the ladder. Simon stayed for one final review, and for the first time his gaze rested on the pile of stones that had once been the floor of the storehouse.

What he saw made him bend for a closer look.

He inspected one stone after another until he had examined all the larger fragments. About half of them were scored and chipped in a way that could never have been caused by their fall. It needed no Sherlock Holmes to deduce how the marks had been caused. Someone had recently been at work on the floor of the storehouse with a pickaxe.

2

That evening he dined alone with Yves Florian and Mimette. Philippe had phoned to say that he would not be home until late, Professor Norbert had pleaded that he wanted to be alone to study the historic implications of the underground chamber, and Henri Pichot and Jeanne Corday were having supper with Gaston at his cottage. As a result the tension that had marked the previous night's meal was absent and the conversation less restricted. After ranging through a wide variety of topics from the state of the franc to the life expectancy of Generalissimo Franco, the talk reverted to the events of the afternoon.

'You must have very extensive cellars here to store your wine,' said the Saint, when he had a suitable opening, and Yves nodded.

'To tell you the truth even I am not certain where they all begin and end, and I have lived here all my life,' Yves confessed. 'My father had new storage facilities built under the courtyard by the *chai*, and it is there that we store most of the wine we produce. Except for the wine we keep for ourselves, which is kept under the kitchens, the old cellars are not used nowadays. Only Gaston, and perhaps Charles, would know all of them.'

'Yesterday on my way from my room to the salon I got lost and ended up at the chapel. I noticed a door at the foot of the stairs, and I assumed that was the main way in.'

'It used to be, but it has not been used for some years. Originally the staircase went right down to the old dungeons of the castle, but they became unsafe, and so we had to brick up the opening and put a door in. I don't suppose anyone has been down there for ten years at least.'

Simon finished the last of his Château Ingare Réserve with unconcealed regret.

'A great wine,' he said. 'You're very generous to let me taste your private stock. I'm surprised the Germans allowed you to keep any of it.'

'We have Gaston and Charles to thank for that. They hid the finest vintages away, I don't know where, and put old labels on all the newest and rawest, and the Boches sat around this very table and praised them to the heavens because he had told them they were so special. But then what can you expect from a nation of beer drinkers?' added Yves with chauvinistic glee.

The Saint wondered what the citizens of Rheinhessen would think of that, but decided not to make the point.

'I suppose Norbert has been pestering Gaston to death about all these closed-off crypts and passages,' he said.

'I have no doubt,' said Yves good-humouredly. 'He is doing no harm, and if he discovers anything of archaeological importance it will be interesting. And Philippe thinks it would do the business no harm to enhance our *snobisme ancestral*.'

'Not to mention my own,' said the Saint lightly.

Mimette put in: 'If you would like to look at our private cellars you would be most welcome. Just see Charles, there is nothing he enjoys more than showing off his private catacombs.'

The Saint was quick to accept.

'Thank you, I should like that very much indeed.'

The next morning after breakfast he took up the offer, and found the family retainer a willing and knowledgeable guide.

Charles ushered him down a winding flight of stone stairs that led off from a corner of a kitchen that looked big enough to prepare three-course meals for a regiment. He had the air of a curator opening the museum vaults to reveal his rarest and most precious collections. He seemed to blend in perfectly with the long racks of cobwebbed bottles and the close musty vinegar smell.

The cellar itself was unremarkable and from Simon's viewpoint something of a disappointment. It consisted of a series of wide interconnecting tunnels that spread like the strands of a spider's web from an open area in the centre, but all the ramifications were ultimately dead ends. The door from the kitchen provided both entrance and exit. At the end of most of the tunnels was a wall of new bricks built to separate the family's personal wine stocks from the rest of the château's cellars.

They walked slowly down the narrow aisles between the racks of bottles. Charles eagerly provided a running commentary on the different wines in his charge and enjoyed answering the Saint's questions in the minutest detail. By the time the tour was completed the Saint's repertoire of wine lore had been substantially increased; while Charles, finding his audience less inept than he had expected, became less formally distant and more congenial.

'You have been at Ingare for a long time?' Simon asked as they returned to the daylight.

'I have always been at Ingare,' answered Charles. 'My father was butler before me, and his father before him. It is so long ago that I am not even sure when he first came here.'

As he carefully double-locked the door to the

cellar, Simon asked: 'What do you think about this treasure of the Templars that everyone is so worked up about?'

'It is not my business,' Charles replied stiffly. 'If there is any, it would belong to the Florians.'

He led the way back into the kitchen and it seemed to the Saint that the further they moved into the house the more Charles became the inscrutable servant and less the wine enthusiast chatting to a fellow connoiseur.

'Perhaps the chamber Gaston fell into yesterday might provide a clue,' Simon ventured. 'I should think there are a number of underground passages here that no one knows about.'

'It is very possible, monsieur,' Charles agreed politely. 'Is there anything else you require?'

There was; but not the kind of domestic service that Charles was offering. The Saint knew when he was being stonewalled and accepted that any further probing would be useless.

That afternoon he visited Gaston. The foreman's home was a white-walled low-roofed cottage at the foot of the hill looking towards the Ouvèze, which he had learnt was the name of the river in the plain below. The ground floor consisted of a single room simply furnished with locally-made furniture. A massive iron stove set into the fireplace served both for heating and for cooking food. The only decorations were an array of shining copper utensils that hung beside the chimney breast and an assortment of framed photographs on the mantelpiece. But despite its spartan appearance the house had a feeling of warmth and security that the château could never project.

Gaston's bed had been brought downstairs and he was sitting propped up in it reading when the Saint arrived.

'I am embarrassed, m'sieur,' he said. 'I have no wounds, but the doctor orders that I must rest for two or three days until the pain in my back is gone.'

The overseer put away his book and the jumble of papers on which he had been scribbling, and for more than an hour they chatted about the harvest weather, about wine-making, about everything and anything but nothing in particular. The only awkward break in the conversation came when Simon brought up the mysterious underground chamber which Gaston had so dramatically and painfully opened up. It was a subject that Gaston gave the impression it would be disloyal or indiscreet of him to discuss.

'That is for the Professor to occupy himself with,' he said gruffly.

As the Saint prepared to leave Gaston became suddenly serious.

'You are still staying at Ingare?'

'Mademoiselle Mimette insists, until my car is

repaired, so I see no reason to leave.'

'Even after what happened to me yesterday?'

'That was the purest accident, wasn't it? Nothing sinister about it. Why should that make me go?'

Gaston did not reply at once. Instead he looked searchingly at his visitor.

'Trust no one,' he cautioned at last. 'Not even those you think of no account.'

'Precisely who do you have in mind?' Simon asked, but the old man was not to be drawn and merely thanked his guest for the visit and bade him a deferential *au revoir*.

On his way back to the château the Saint stopped at the tower. The scene was the same as it had been when the séance broke up. The table, the overturned chairs, the circle of cards and the shattered wine glass at the foot of the column had not been picked up or moved. He searched for several minutes before finding what he was looking for. The piece of thread was almost hidden in a crack between the flagstones. Simon extracted it with care and slipped it into an envelope in his pocket. He continued on his way to the château, leaving everything else exactly as it had been.

'I must stop reading detective stories,' he told himself.

It is said that before an earthquake you can hear the silence. The animals and birds depart, only the people remain unaware. The Saint, whose instinct for danger was as finely honed as any animal's watched the behaviour of his companions with a naturalist's detachment during the following two days.

The events of the preceding forty-eight hours were treated with well-bred indifference, as if ignoring them would make them go away. In the same manner his presence became accepted, and he realised how Norbert had managed to turn a weekend visit into a six-week stay. Conventional references to the condition of his car were easily and deftly coped with.

Supplied with the morsels of information the Saint had gathered during his brief stay at Château Ingare, any ordinary private investigator would have exhausted himself trying to unravel the spaghetti of riddles that providence had heaped on his plate, until he and everyone else around was suffering from acute indigestion. The Saint did not. In fact to any observer unfamiliar with his methods he appeared to do nothing at all.

After the excitement generated by Gaston Pichot's accidental discovery of the underground chamber had subsided, life at the château returned to as near normal as its motley assortment of personalities would allow, and Simon slipped comfortably into the routine of the household. The time-honoured ritual of the harvest continued, and he followed the progress of the grapes from vine to press to fermenting

144

vat with genuine interest. When not in the fields or watching the wine being made he behaved exactly as any other guest would have done.

Philippe Florian had returned from Avignon and appointed himself to take charge of the Hecate crypt. His archaeological interest was negligible; but his keenness to facilitate Louis Norbert's study of it was very great. Since every able-bodied worker on the *domaine* was fully occupied with the picking and processing of grapes, he took on the task of securing the safety of the rest of the ceiling himself, revealing unsuspected talents as a practical handyman. With the professor fluttering around to fetch and carry and lend an unmuscular hand, he brought in planks and timber and did a very competent job of underpinning the floor above. The scraping of his saw and the hammering of wedges reverberated to the outside for hours at a time.

For his part, Simon was unobtrusive to the point of elusiveness. Jeanne Corday's clothes and poses placed her in the centre of the spotlight he had previously occupied, and he was content to fade into the background and watch and wait.

After dinner on the fourth day following his arrival, all the others excused themselves early for one reason or another, and for the first time in a long while he found himself alone again with Mimette in the salon.

She wasted no time in taking advantage of the opportunity.

'You must have a lot to tell me.'

It was so close to sounding like an imperious challenge that he was amused to treat it with elaborate carelessness.

'Not really—why should I?'

A slight flush tinged the girl's cheeks.

'You mean you've been doing nothing?'

'I can't say I've been a great help with the *récolte*,' Simon granted. 'And Philippe already has an enthusiastic assistant.'

'Which should have left you plenty of time to do something else useful.'

'What would you have proposed?' he teased her lazily. 'Should I have brought in a steam shovel and started digging up your foundations until we found a treasure which may not even exist?'

'You know there is something wrong here, and I thought you were going to try to discover it.'

Suddenly she sounded very tired and lonely, and the Saint relented.

'Okay,' he said. 'I'd like to show you something. Can we go back to the dining-room?'

Wonderingly, but without hesitation, she moved to the door.

The dining-room, meticulously cleared of all trace of dinner, looked stark and lifeless in the blaze that she switched on. Simon put a match to a single one of the candles in the massive silver candelabrum on the sideboard, and turned off the electricity.

'There, that's a lot better,' he said. 'More atmospheric and *misterioso*. Now, would you sneak into the nether regions and fetch us a large wine glass. Empty.'

'But why?'

'I'm going to show you a party trick that I happened to remember.'

When she returned, he had laid out a rough circle of torn pieces of paper at one end of the table top, which he was lightly polishing with a silk handkerchief.

'Of course, Charles keeps this table waxed and shined like a flies' skating rink,' he remarked, 'which makes the trick much easier.' He placed the glass upside-down in the centre of the paper circle and tested its mobility with a finger-tip. 'Now, you sit down opposite me—'

'What is this—another séance?'

'With a difference. But we might as well get in the mood.'

As she reluctantly took the chair across from him, he went on:

'I've been making use of your library, swotting up on the history of your noble house.'

'And?'

'Your ancestors—and maybe mine—seem to have been a pretty barbaric crowd even for those days. It seems that one of the first Florians, who had rashly promised some characters that they would not be hurt, kept them in the dungeons beneath this very room and simply starved them to death. But every day he had a sumptuous meal prepared and placed outside their cells— just out of reach. "They must not be allowed to believe," he said, "that I am starving them to save money.""'

Mimette grimaced. 'How horrible!'

'Of course, if you weren't feeling subtle, there were always the good old fun things to do, like one master of Ingare who used any peasants who complained for crossbow practice.'

'That was a different age, a different world,' she said defensively. 'It can't be blamed on the Florians of today.'

'In another thirty years the Germans will be saying the same about the Nazis. And I suppose they'll be right, too,' said the Saint philosophically. 'All the same, it does make this a place where a spiritualist could expect a good crop of spooks. I wonder how many men have entered Ingare and never left? Just think of the cries of despair and the screams of agony these walls must have heard, the murder and mayhem they must have seen . . .'

'I don't want to think about it,' said Mimette obdurately.

She looked at the scraps of paper that he had laid out, and said: 'Anyhow, these are all blank, so how is your spook going to communicate?'

148

'I hope the problem will drive him crazy,' Simon said happily. 'Now let's see if we can make contact. Put your finger on the glass.'

The Saint's voice was quietly authoritative and Mimette obeyed.

In a few moments the glass moved a little.

She looked at him sharply.

'You're cheating!'

'I am not.'

The movements became more pronounced and erratic.

'According to unbelievers,' Simon said steadily, 'one of the players eventually, intentionally or involuntarily, gives the glass a tiny push. The others feel it, and unconsciously resist it or try to change its direction. The conflict of forces leads to stronger and wider movements as the pressures get more unbalanced...'

Even while he was explaining it, the glass began to move more definitely about the table.

The Saint asked no questions as Norbert had done, but simply allowed the glass to go where it seemed to want to. Mimette followed its peregrinations as if mesmerised. The glass moved faster and faster until it was darting to one point after another on the circle of paper scraps.

'Now are *you* cheating?' Simon challenged.

As he expected, she snatched her finger indignantly off the glass. The Saint immediately followed suit. But the glass did not stop.

For a few seconds longer it went on moving as if it had a will of its own, until with gathering speed it flew straight off the edge of the table into the surrounding gloom.

'Well,' drawled the Saint, 'I guess not finding any letters to spell with did drive our spook of the evening up the wall.'

Mimette had barely stifled a scream. She stared at Simon in wide-eyed disbelief and then ran and switched on the lights. Grinning, the Saint picked up the glass and replaced it on the table before blowing out the candle and collecting his pieces of paper.

Mimette remained standing by the light switch. She was deathly pale and her hands were clasped tightly together to stop them shaking. Despite her efforts at self control her voice shook.

'It was a trick!' she babbled. 'It must have been a trick!'

'It was,' he said cheerfully. 'As I told myself when I saw it in the tower. And like most good tricks, so easy once you know how.'

'Please,' she implored. 'What did you do?'

On the sideboard there was also an antique silver carrying-stand with a set of small stemless glasses in sockets around its base and a cut crystal decanter in the centre. The decanter held a liquid of encouragingly amber tint. Simon unstoppered it, sniffed the heady aroma of old

150

marc, and poured two generous restorative shots. He handed one to Mimette before continuing.

'It's all so obvious, really—straight out of the Amateur Sorcerer's Handbook. First create an atmosphere, which is even easier if you have an old tower once occupied by Satanic knights. Enhance said atmosphere with lack of light. Then make sure everyone is concentrating as hard as possible because when you stare too hard at something for too long you end up not really seeing it at all. That's why a conjuror always tells you to watch closely—what he wants you to watch. Then it's easy to perform the required legerdemain.'

'But that glass moved by itself, when we weren't touching it,' protested Mimette. 'So did the one at the seance in the tower.'

'Not quite,' said the Saint.

He held up a single strand of black thread knotted at one end.

'Take a highly polished table and wine glass, give the rim of the glass a film of oil perhaps, just with a fingertip from your own hair, and the glass will move at the lightest of touches. The pressure it needs is so slight that even the others who have a finger on the glass can't detect who is starting it. When the glass comes to the edge of the table, slip the thread under the rim and the knot will keep it there. In semi-darkness it's as good as invisible. When the time is right give

151

the thread a quick tug and the glass flies off the table. Like I said, so simple when you know.'

'But who would go to all that trouble? And why?' she puzzled, and Simon shrugged.

'*Who* is easy. It's the *why* that baffles me.'

'Who, then?'

'If you remember, the glass left the table and hit the pillar I was standing behind. Norbert was sitting at one end of the table and Philippe was facing me. That only leaves one person who was in exactly the right place.'

3

Mimette's brow furrowed as she worked out the solution. She gave a short and uncertain laugh.

'Henri? Don't be silly!'

Simon was unmoved.

'The limitation of that trick is that you can only move the glass towards you, or a little to one side, as you pull the thread under the edge of the table. Henri was the only one in a position to send it the way it went.'

She seemed to make an effort to remain sceptical.

'But why should Henri go to all that trouble?'

'That, as Hamlet always said, is the question,' Simon shrugged. 'Perhaps he's a secret practical joker.'

'Not Henri.'

'I didn't think so. If the glass hadn't smashed against the column, and brought me into the act, we might have found out. He couldn't have known that I was standing there, so it was pure bad luck that I broke up the proceedings just as you made your appearance.'

'What are we going to do about it?' demanded Mimette.

The Saint lifted one free hand and shoulder.

'Nothing.'

'Nothing!'

'It's no crime to fake a séance,' he contended.

'But no one would do it without a dishonest reason.'

'Did I have a dishonest reason just now?'

'No, but you—Oh! You—you—'

She was almost spluttering with feminine exasperation at the idiocy of masculine logic.

The Saint was wise enough not to try to score any more intellectual points.

'All we have at the moment is a good reason to keep an eye on Henri,' he said quietly. 'And we'll have a much better chance of spotting something more if he doesn't know he's being watched. So just for now, will you keep my little demonstration private, between the two of us?'

Mimette frowned.

'*Excusez-moi.*' The words were difficult for her to say. 'I have no right to speak to you as if I had hired you. It's only because, since you came here, I've been hoping so much—'

'And believe me, Mimette,' he said steadily, 'I'm hoping I won't let you down.'

She looked up at him uncertainly, desperately wanting to believe. Simon Templar looked down into her dark troubled eyes and put down his glass. Before she realised what was happening, his lips were against hers. Her eyes opened wide in astonishment for a moment, but only for a moment. Slowly they closed as the tension dissolved, and she relaxed gratefully into the security of his arms.

As usual the following morning Simon breakfasted alone. Those with work to do were busy doing it, while Jeanne Corday's ideas on the proper time for reveille were even more sybaritic than his own. Today however he knew that there would be a surfeit of conviviality to make up for it later. The last of the grapes would be brought in that afternoon, and in the evening there would be the traditional party for all who had worked on the harvest.

He was looking forward to the festivities. Not simply because they would be enjoyable in themselves, but because it would be his first opportunity to observe all the Florian clan and their cohorts in the informal bustle of a sociable free-for-all—which might provide an interesting floor show.

A stroll around the château grounds after breakfast had become something of a ritual and that morning his route took him first towards the *chai* and its dependent storehouse. In the cobbled courtyard which they partly enclosed he found Gaston Pichot leaning on a stout stick and watching a mound of laden baskets being carried in from the truck.

'These are the *Petit Syrah*,' Gaston explained. 'Blended in our own proportion with the usual Cabernet grapes, they are what give the wines of Ingare their unique flavour.'

'I'm glad to see you're on the job again,' said the Saint sincerely. 'And feeling a lot better?'

'I could have felt so much worse,' said the indomitable old man. 'But I was born in a good year. My vintage has outlasted many younger ones, and it will outlast many more. We have a proverb in Provençale: *Vau miès pourta lou dou que lou linçou*—it is better to wear the mourning than the coffin.'

'I shall adopt that as my motto,' Simon laughed. '*A bientôt, mon ami.*'

He sauntered on, around to the storehouse where Gaston had literally stumbled into one of the long-lost secrets of the château.

The floor was now securely pit-propped and the ladder had been solidly braced so that it practically became a steep flight of stairs. The debris had been removed and a cable run from the generator in the adjoining pressing house supplied power for a couple of light bulbs.

Unexpectedly, the underground chamber was temporarily deserted. Since its discovery Norbert had virtually lived there, leaving it reluctantly only for hurried meals and snatched

155

sleep. Reasoning that even professors are subject to the dictates of nature, Simon decided to wait for Norbert to return.

The statue looked somehow less sinister in the unglamorous glare of three hundred watts than it had in the wavering flashlights. As he stood beside it facing the chilling emptiness of its eyes, he saw that it was not set flush against the wall as he had originally supposed. Only the plinth was attached to the wall, but the figure centered on it was well clear. A fetishist, if so inclined, could have put his arms around its horrors and embraced it.

The Saint did almost that, but with the purely idle object of testing whether the statue was integrated with its base or merely planted on it.

And the statue moved, with an ease quite disproportionate to the effort he had applied with respect to its presumable weight. In fact, so smoothly that he was momentarily thrown off balance. It was as if the statue had responded by coming to life in weird co-operation. And to add to the eeriness of the effect, a ghostly squeak and clink of chain whined through the chamber, while he had a visual hallucination of a part of the wall within his field of vision moving away from him.

As he regained his footing, both physically and intellectually, he realised that the wall actually had moved. In fact, a whole section of masonry had turned, in perfect synchronisation

156

with the turning of the statue, opening a door into a passageway that instantly lost itself in total darkness.

Long afterwards, he would be profoundly impressed by the technical sophistication that was evidenced by the smooth working of the secret mechanism. After so many hundred years, anything made of iron or steel would have been rusted into permanent immovability. Yet bronze was an alloy that had been known even in the great days of the Château Ingare, although few engineers of the era seem to have concerned themselves with the problems of corrosion. The Templars who had installed that shrine of Hecate must have been centuries ahead of the thinking of their contemporaries, and what they built had been designed to outlast themselves by tens of generations.

But for those first moments, the Saint was too startled by his own discovery to stop and marvel at the technology which had made it possible. He took a deep breath and exhaled it in a long low whistle as he waited for his pulse rate to slow and a sense of reality to return and shuffle the jumbled sensations of the past seconds into a semblance of order.

That done, he walked over to the opening and peered cautiously in. The light from the bulbs in the crypt reached just far enough into the narrow passage to show that it was cut through the natural rock of the hillside and the stone blocks of the pivoting secret door were only a few inches thick.

The door had not swung completely open but stood about two feet ajar. A heavy chain ran around a toothed wheel at the bottom corner of the door, through the wall and into the base of the statue, where there would have to be another similar wheel. As one turned, so would the other. Simple but perfectly effective, and it still worked.

Two steps into the passage and he blocked his own light, making it impossible to see even inches ahead, and he returned to the chamber to cast around in the vain hope that a torch might have been left there.

Then he heard a movement somewhere above, and moved swiftly back to the statue. The creak of the chain as he turned the figure back to close the stone panel again sounded deafeningly loud to him in the confined space.

He need not have worried. Perhaps Louis Norbert was too engrossed in his own thoughts, perhaps he was slightly hard of hearing, or perhaps he was even a superb poker player, but whatever the reason he gave no indication of having heard anything unusual when he stepped from the ladder.

He regarded the Saint with a mixture of irritation and suspicion.

'Monsieur Templar. Were you looking for me?'

Simon uncrossed his legs and rose from the stone bench where he had hastily seated himself. The door had closed so perfectly that had he not known exactly where it was he would never have been able to guess. Even so, he kept his eyes away from the wall as he smiled amiably at the little professor.

'Not specially,' he said. 'But it's a pleasure to see you. You haven't been very social since this hole was opened.'

'What can I do for you?' Norbert enquired in the politely uninterested tone of a shop assistant.

'I just dropped in to see how you were getting along,' Simon replied pleasantly.

Norbert scratched at the tuft of white hair that stuck out above his left ear. He looked tired and his clothes were crumpled. The collar of his shirt curled at the edges and the front of it was smeared with grime. He had the general appearance of a man who had spent the night on a park bench.

He continued to fix the Saint with an inquisitorial glare. Simon waved a hand towards the marble goddess.

'Has horrible Hecate told you anything yet?' he asked. 'Opened up any new avenues of investigation?'

'No. Why should it? It's just a very interesting work of ancient art,' Norbert said defensively.

'*Vraiment?*'

The Saint drawled the word so slowly and with such an inflection of cynical reverence that Professor Norbert flinched.

'I am just trying to make my studies,' he stammered, wrenching his gaze away and trying instead to concentrate on opening the carpenter's rule he took from his pocket. 'But trivial distractions make my task so much harder.'

Simon took the rule from his fumbling fingers and opened it out to its full length. He looked from Norbert to the statue and back again, and then proffered the metre of wood to the other's hand like a general presenting a sword.

'I hope she measures up to your expectations,' he said suggestively; and while Norbert was trying to work out a *double entendre* Simon patted him encouragingly on the shoulder and leisurely climbed the ladder to the storehouse above.

Which in its own way was as good an exit as the circumstances allowed, he reflected as he made his way back to the château. He would have wished for more time to follow up his own discovery, but was sufficiently grateful that the Professor's fortuitous absence had allowed him the time to make it.

The question was, had Norbert long since beaten him to it? And where did that melodramatically hidden doorway lead?

The Saint would have to find some more answers for himself, which foreshadowed a possibly sleepless night of further exploring when he would be better equipped for the excursion.

He re-entered the château through the kitchens with the intention of going to the library to continue his struggle with the medieval French of the Templar records, but a sound of voices from the dining-room stopped him.

They were raised to that pitch just below shouting which is the key of an argument that is about to crescendo into a row. Simon tiptoed noiselessly over and stood with his ear against the door. There was no need to look through the keyhole to identify the contestants, for the more forceful of the two voices could only belong to Jeanne Corday, while the other defiantly apologetic tones were undoubtedly those of Henri Pichot.

'Yes sir, no sir! What sort of man are you?' the girl was sneering. 'They treat you like a guest, and you treat them as if you were a servant.'

'It is not like that,' Henri whined. 'There are ways of doing things. You do not understand them like I do.'

'You mean I don't curtsey every time they walk into a room?'

'It is not as simple as that,' Henri protested. 'I

161

must be careful. I am doing everything I can.'

'If you were half the man Philippe is, everything would be settled by now,' his fiancée countered spitefully. 'In two days I am going back to Paris. With or without your cheap ring.'

'But you said . . .'

'With or without your ring,' Jeanne repeated coldly. 'It's up to you.'

Simon just had time to move back from the door before it was flung open. Jeanne Corday stormed past him without acknowledgment. Henri stood gaping dumbly at her retreating figure.

'A lovers' tiff?' Simon asked sympathetically, and the lawyer rounded on him with uncharacteristic violence.

'Go to hell,' he snarled, and hurried after his lady love.

Simon found Pascal and Jules on the vineyard slopes, and shared an alfresco worker's lunch with them before excusing himself for the private siesta which he felt that his constitution required.

Soon after six o'clock, refreshingly bathed and very casually spruced up, he made his way back down towards the *chai*.

The huddle of outbuildings formed three sides of a rectangle with the fourth side open to a panoramic view of the valley. The party was prepared in the courtyard between the buildings. Two long trestle tables had been loaded with eatables and wooden benches placed against the walls. Empty barrels served as extra tables or chairs as the occasion demanded. A couple of large casks had been set out on stands, and the permanent and seasonal toilers of the vineyard were already busy sampling the wine they had made the year before.

Yves and Mimette strolled from group to group, chatting hospitably. Philippe stood a little apart from the crowd, a slightly condescending smile playing at the corner of his mouth as he sipped his wine. Henri and Jeanne Corday sat together on one of the benches without speaking. It was plain from the stiffness of their poses and the lack of conversation that their tempers had not cooled since the morning. There was no sign of either Gaston or Professor Norbert. The Saint had not expected the Professor to leave his work for such frivolity, but he was surprised that the old foreman was not yet present.

As he stood and surveyed the scene, he discovered Pascal and Jules, and was about to walk over and join them when Jeanne Corday rose and hurried across towards him. Henri gazed sullenly after her but made no move to follow.

She was wearing a blouse that was intended to appear two sizes too small. The matching green skirt was equally tight and equally brief. The conversation of the two students might have

163

proved more intelligent, but the Saint was only human. He bestowed his most dazzling smile on her. It was returned with a flash of polar white caps.

'*Alors, vous voici,*' she greeted brightly. 'Among the peasants.'

'*Vous aussi,*' Simon responded. 'Enjoying yourself?'

'Are you kidding?'

Her eyes flicked shamelessly over him and he returned the compliment with an equally brazen appraisal.

'What's the matter?'

Jeanne sighed wearily and sipped her drink. It was not the colour of wine, and he suspected that it was stronger.

'I mean, it's all very nice here, but it's so quiet, so open, just fields and things. I mean, it's so . . .'

'Rural,' suggested the Saint helpfully.

'*Ouais,* well, something like that,' she agreed with a shrug.

'But you're going back to the bright lights soon. Paris in two days, isn't it?'

'Of course, you heard that,' said Jeanne, momentarily disconcerted. She recovered quickly. 'I mean, Henri is wonderful, but he acts differently down here. In Paris he's amusing, but around this place he creeps about as if he was a lackey or something. I know the family have been good to him, but—'

'They make him feel inferior? I'm sure they don't mean to.'

'You would not know how to feel like that, would you?'

'I'm too stupid to be sensitive,' said the Saint disarmingly. 'But don't you agree that it makes life more comfortable?'

Jeanne looked uncertain whether she was the butt of some subtle joke, but she did not let it bother her for long.

'I heard you were on your way to Paris when you got stuck here. If you ever make it, you must look me up. We could have some fun,' she added transparently.

Simon gave the idea a few seconds' serious consideration.

'You know,' he said judiciously, 'I do believe we could.'

He had been watching Henri out of the corner of his eye. The young lawyer had not taken his eyes off them. Finally unable to endure the scene any longer, he came over. He ignored the Saint and addressed his fiancée.

'I think we'd better circulate,' he said brusquely.

Jeanne contemplated him with distaste.

'Circulate? What do you think I am—some sort of blood corpuscle?' she jeered, and Henri's cheeks turned a rich shade of crimson.

Without a word he turned and strode away towards the château. Jeanne smiled as she rested a hand on the Saint's shoulder and moved closer.

'This is boring,' she said silkily. 'Why don't we go pick some grapes on our own?'

Simon felt a very natural temptation to do just that. Whether or not he would have succumbed to it was never to be known, for at that moment one of the workmen rushed from the building behind the Saint and almost bowled him over as he half ran, half staggered across the cobbles shouting for Yves.

'Excuse me,' said the Saint abruptly and went after him.

The man was in a state of shock. His words spilled out in an incoherent babble. He stood with one shaking arm pointing towards the building he had come from.

'Routine check... lifted lid... lying there... Gaston...'

Yves Florian was trying bewilderedly to make sense of the words but the Saint preferred action. He spun round and sprinted into the building, more than half dreading what he was going to see.

It was the place used for the first fermentation of the newly pressed wine. Inside were a dozen huge vats, each taller than a man and linked by a narrow catwalk reached by a flight of steps. The heavy lid had been dragged from one of the vats and stood propped against the side. The Saint raced up to the catwalk and made for the open tank. He peered over the rim and looked down into the thick red pulpy liquid. The sightless eyes of Gaston Pichot returned his stare.

4

The Saint turned, to find Philippe the first to arrive beside him, followed by three or four of the château workers, while the rest of the harvest party were crowding in on the floor below. Simon spoke to them all.

'*C'est vrai*,' he said. '*Gaston est mort.*'

At first, a numbness of shocked disbelief seemed to make them refuse to accept that such a thing could happen there. The silence was stifling in its intensity as the assembled onlookers stood staring, unable to drive their minds past the news they had been given.

Simon looked down again at the limp figure that was half submerged in the blood-coloured wine. He had developed a genuine affection and respect for the old man, but there would be a time for sadness later, just as there would be a time for retribution. It was the unemotional practicalities that had to be dealt with now, and Philippe set the process in motion while Yves was still climbing up to the catwalk.

'Mimette, go with Jeanne to the château and telephone the *gendarmerie*. Someone give me a hand to get Gaston out.'

The sharp authority of his voice reawakened the others as suddenly as if a switch had been thrown.

The two women hurried out together, relieved that they would not have to watch the grisly scene of the body being moved. Without bothering to remove his jacket, Philippe himself leaned into the vat and grabbed Gaston by the lapels of his coat. Simon gripped his ankles, and together they lifted him out and carried him down to the floor, where someone had spread a tarpaulin.

Philippe allowed no flicker of emotion to show on his face and betray his feelings. He gave the impression of knowing what had to be done and getting on with it however distasteful it might be. After putting Gaston down, he simply turned away in search of a rag to dry his hands.

The Saint was well aware of the dictum that nothing should be touched until the police have inspected the scene of the crime, but it was not for him to argue with Philippe's orders. He was also aware that the local gendarme would be unlikely to have much experience in examining murder victims. Since the body had been moved anyway, he took the further liberty of feeling around its head and testing the stiffness of the joints, and understood what his fingers told him. He looked at the soles of the old man's boots and at the dirt under his fingernails. At last he folded the ends of the tarpaulin over the body and straightened up.

'*Pauvre Gaston!*' Yves was muttering, literally

wringing his hands. 'How could it have happened? If he slipped and fell in—'

'He wouldn't have drowned so peacefully,' said the Saint.

'Perhaps a heart attack?'

'Caused by a clout on the head,' Simon said grimly. 'There's a dent in his skull you could stick your thumb into.'

Yves's face was white and his lips trembled as he gazed at the makeshift shroud.

'But who would do that?' he asked brokenly.

'We'll find out,' said the Saint, injecting his voice with an assurance that made it a promise. 'But there's nothing more I can do here for the moment. Will you excuse me for a few minutes?'

Without waiting for formal permission, he eased his way out of the building through the throng of employees, who had now split into small groups and were chattering excitedly in hushed tones.

Heading back towards the château, he met Mimette returning towards the *chai*.

'Jeanne is waiting to meet the police,' she told him before he had time to ask.

'Good. I was scheming to get you away. Come with me.'

'Where to?'

'Gaston's house.'

They took Mimette's Renault. The Saint drove, throwing the car down the rutted track towards the foreman's cottage as if he begrudged every second's delay.

'Why Gaston's?' shouted Mimette, trying to make her voice heard above the roar of the engine as she clung to the edge of the door to save being hurled clear as they bounced over the washboard road.

'Because that was where Gaston was probably murdered,' Simon answered.

'But it was an accident,' Mimette protested, uncertainly.

The Saint shook his head. He pulled the car to a skidding stop outside the cottage and jumped out.

'He was dead long before he was dumped into the vat,' he said brutally. 'Someone hit him very hard on the back of the head with what the police like to call a blunt instrument. It was meant to look like an accident, but very crudely done. I hate amateur murderers—they are an insult to the craft.'

The door was unlocked, and the Saint pushed it wide with his foot while holding Mimette back.

It was not booby trapped, but the room was a shambles. The mattress and cushions from the bed had been ripped open and their stuffings scattered across the floor, even the stove had been emptied and the ashes sifted through. While Mimette stood in the doorway and surveyed the chaos Simon went around the room checking on the details.

Beside the bed, in a sea of papers, photographs and torn books, lay an upturned trunk. Simon picked up a handful of papers and glanced through them. They were the ephemera of a long life—a discharge certificate from the first war and a ration book from the second, letters and greetings cards from relatives and friends, an insurance policy that had long since lapsed.

Mimette took a few hesitant steps into the room and stood watching him.

'What are you looking for?'

Simon tossed the papers back on to the floor.

'I'm not quite sure, but I think it's what detectives call a clue.' He regarded his surroundings wryly. 'But I think our villain has been too thorough—messy but effective.'

Mimette nodded towards the fireplace. In the bottom right-hand corner four bricks had been removed. In the grate lay a small leather sachet.

'Even Gaston's cubbyhole,' she sighed, and picked up the wallet.

She gasped as she lifted the flap, and the Saint reached over and took it from her. Inside were bundles of notes, many so old that they were no longer legal tender.

'How did you know where Gaston hid his money?' he asked.

'I didn't, at least I didn't know it was money he kept there. Once, when I was a child, I ran in and he was putting the sachet into that hole. He was very cross that I'd seen him. He said it was a secret place, and made me swear never to tell anyone.'

'And did you?'

Mimette sighed.

'Oh, I don't remember. It was so long ago. I'd forgotten all about it until now. Don't you think it's strange that the murderer should have left the money behind?'

'It just means that not only is he an amateur but he's a very amateurish amateur,' Simon replied as he replaced the wallet in the grate. 'If he'd had any sense he would have at least made it look like a robbery.'

She waved her hand over the litter around them.

'But if he wasn't looking for money, what did he want?'

Simon was about to turn away from the fireplace when a scrap of yellow among the grey ashes caught his eye. He brushed them aside and retrieved a tiny piece of parchment.

'I should think,' he said slowly, 'that he wanted the rest of this.'

It was made from the same material as the scraps he had seen in the casket under the statue of Hecate. Its triangular shape suggested that it had once been a corner of a page. On it were drawn two vertical, parallel lines behind which was a circle. A third line zig-zagged beneath

172

them.

Mimette peered over his shoulder as he studied his find.

'But what is it?' she asked.

'It's why Gaston was killed,' he answered, and forestalled the inevitable questions by heading for the car. 'I'll explain on the way back to the château.'

Their return was undertaken at a speed more suited to the state of the road and the limitations of the car, and as they drove he told her what had happened after Gaston had fallen into the chamber under the storehouse.

'I heard him moving about and when I got down there I found that the box under the statue had recently been broken open. Everything but the lid of the box was covered in dust and the scratches on the lock were new. I was sure Gaston must have opened it; but if he'd taken something out, short of searching him there wasn't anything I could do. I thought then that it might have been some sort of document, and now I'm sure of it.'

'And that's what the murderer wanted?'

'It must have been.'

'But how did he know Gaston had it?'

'By making the same deduction that I made, from the evidence in the crypt. And the only reason he'd be prepared to kill for it would be if it was very valuable or the key to something valuable . . .'

173

'The treasure!'

'Right in one. I don't know how this bit was torn off. It could have happened during a struggle or when it was pulled out of its hiding place.'

'But if the murderer has the rest of the parchment he will find the treasure,' said Mimette despairingly.

'Maybe, maybe not,' said the Saint. 'It depends whether he understands it. Even if he does, he won't be able to just pick up the loot and walk away. At any rate, it doesn't seem as if Gaston could have.'

There was a few seconds' pause, and then she said: 'Why do you think Gaston was keeping this to himself?'

'That,' said the Saint dourly, 'is one question I wish we didn't have to think about.'

As a temporary evasion, he took the scrap of parchment from his pocket and handed it to her.

'Does this mean anything to you?'

Mimette shook her head as she studied it, turning it this way and that.

'Not a thing. I suppose those two upright lines could represent a building, but I can't think what the squiggly line or the circle could mean.' She handed it back with a shrug of apology. 'I'm sorry.'

The shadows were lengthening, casting the hillside into a purple twilight as the sun sank behind the other side of the ridge, but it was not artistic appreciation of the sunset that sparked an idea in Simon's mind. When they stopped in the shade of the château it had crystallised.

'How about this for a guess,' he suggested. 'If the two vertical lines could represent a building, then the circle could represent the sun.'

'But what would that mean?' asked his bemused companion.

'It identifies the building. The sun is behind it, so it's either setting or rising. The building must be in either the west or the east. Now, the west wing of the château is the most modern part and there's nothing there that this could represent. But on the east side—'

'There's the tower!' Mimette finished for him excitedly. But her elation lasted only a moment. 'It still doesn't tell us anything.'

'It's a starting point, anyhow,' said the Saint.

He had a sudden glimpse of a police car swinging off the main driveway to brake in front of the house with an impressive squeal of tyres, and slid lower in his seat.

'The law has arrived,' he said. 'You'd better go meet them. I'll be along in a minute—there's just something I'd like to check on first.'

As she started to get out of the car he reached across and squeezed her arm reassuringly.

'Don't tell anybody where we've been. This is our party and we don't want the gendarmes gatecrashing it. OK?'

'*Si vous y tenez*,' replied Mimette hesitantly.

175

'I do. And trust me. Everything is going to be all right.'

'I hope so,' said the girl fervently.

Simon waited until the forecourt was deserted before leaving the car and heading directly for the tower.

He inspected the walls and floor carefully before beginning to climb the stairs to the battlements. Halfway up he rested and glanced down. As far as he was able to judge he was standing on what would once have been the landing of the second storey. He stood on a level with the top of the column and noticed that protruding from the top of it were three buttresses intricately carved with gargoyles whose fearsomeness had been smoothed away by the wind and rain of centuries. As a trio, they reflected the symbolic faces of Hecate, the *Regina* of Ingare.

He stood on the narrow ledge that circled the inside of the walls and looked out over the battlements. From his vantage point he could look down on every part of the château and its grounds, and across the plain below to the steely ribbon of the Ouvèze. He rested his elbows on the top of the wall and idly wondered how much the view had changed since the last sentry of the Knights Templar had stood in the same spot so many hundreds of years before.

Somewhere within his purview must be the place that the rest of that piece of parchment had been intended to pinpoint. But what real chance was there of locating it from the fragment in his possession?

He was abruptly snapped out of his thoughts by the sound of footsteps reaching the top of the stairway. Startled from his reverie, he turned sharply and in doing so pressed his weight against the wall. Cracked by the frosts of six hundred winters the stone blocks were no longer up to the sudden strain. With a sound like the rumble of distant thunder they crashed outwards.

For one giddy instant the Saint stood poised on the edge of nothing before his feet slipped from the crumbling edge and he pitched down into space.

CHAPTER FIVE

HOW SERGEANT OLIVET TRIED TO COPE, AND MIMETTE WAS NOT ALTOGETHER IMPARTIAL

The gravitational velocity of the Saint's fall adjusted by his aerodynamic resistance should have deposited him in an ungainly and lifeless heap at the foot of the tower precisely 1.38 seconds after his feet slipped off the ramparts.

But speed, as any physicist worthy of his theorems will explain, is relative, and in matters of self-preservation the Saint's brain functioned in an overdrive that threatened to smash the light barrier.

The stone blocks forming the castellations of the battlements broke outwards, but the Saint dropped straight down with his legs actually brushing the wall. Shock, dismay, fear, were all experienced and controlled in the instant it took for sixty of his seventy-four inches to pass below the level of the walkway.

At the moment of collapse he had instinctively flung his arms out in a vain attempt to maintain his balance, so that as the side of the tower flashed by his fingers were already spread and bent, raking the air. His hands smacked against the top of the wall and somehow found something solid, and he winced as his shoulders took the sudden strain. His whole body stiffened and jerked outwards. For one giddy instant the earth seemed to tilt to meet him as the tower leant over towards a slanting horizon before he swung back and hit the wall with a jolt that might easily have dislodged his haphazard grip, but his fingers held on as stubbornly as steel grappling hooks.

He hung motionless and waited. His face was pressed against the wall and he was careful not to look down or think of the void below. As the seconds slipped away he was chilled by a new coldness that owed nothing to the freshening breeze.

Whoever had been following him could not have failed to see him fall. Now he was totally defenceless and at the mercy of anyone on the parapet.

Carefully he tested the resistance of the weakened stone by shifting his weight first on to his left hand and then on to his right. Satisfied that there was a better than even chance of it taking the strain, he began to pull himself slowly up. His feet scraped the wall, seeking extra leverage from the cracks where the mortar had crumbled.

Inch by inch he hoisted his body higher, and as he did so he heard the footsteps again. They had been only a few yards behind him when the battlements had collapsed, but now the sound came from farther away and was growing fainter with every step.

The Saint smiled grimly.

'Going to pick up the pieces, are we?' he murmured, as his waist came level with the top of the wall. 'Well, we'll see.'

He kicked out, at the same time pushing down on the palms of his hands and throwing himself forward, and tumbled over on to the safety of the parapet.

The dusk was rapidly deepening into night, but the moon and stars were still too low in the sky to help him as he peered into the gloom

179

below. He could just make out a figure nearing the bottom of the stairs, but the darkness and the distance between them made identification impossible.

Crouched low to avoid being silhouetted against the sky, he reached the top of the staircase and went down with the speed and surefootedness of a mountain cat. He hardly glanced at the steps as he watched the figure reach the floor and begin to walk towards the door.

The Saint increased his speed, and as he gained the final flight he saw the figure stop and look up.

He covered the remaining steps three at a time, jumping the last half dozen, and landed within arm's length of Louis Norbert.

'*Bon soir*,' said the Saint with rigid politeness, and Norbert reeled back as if he had been struck.

His face was as pale as wax and he stared incredulously at Simon.

'But I thought . . .'

His voice trailed away as the Saint took a step nearer.

'Yes?' prompted the Saint coldly. 'You thought?'

'That—that you had fallen. I saw you. I was going to see . . . that is . . . if you were . . .' Again the words died in Norbert's throat as he stood and gaped at the Saint.

'If I'd saved you the trouble of pushing me?'

Simon took another pace forward, and Norbert retreated until he felt the column at his back and was forced to stop and continue to face the Saint.

The professor shook his head vigorously and stammered: 'No, no, you're wrong! I wasn't... why should I... You can't think that—'

'Why can't I?' Simon enquired reasonably, and Norbert flinched at the mockery in his voice. 'I didn't see you rushing to the rescue.'

Norbert wiped his hand across a forehead that was suddenly cold and damp.

'But I thought you had fallen. How could I know? You must believe me,' he whined.

'Must I? You took your time getting down.'

'I was confused. Scared. I waited. I did not know what to do. Then I decided I had better come down to see if you were... if there was anything I could do. To get help.'

'Of course, you just happened to be around. You weren't following me, were you? Until I fell, you probably didn't even notice me. Right?'

'No. I mean yes—that is, I saw you go into the tower and I came after you. The police want to talk to all of us. I came to tell you. That is all. I swear it. It is the truth. That was the only reason.'

The Saint regarded the twitching scholar without pity. He put out a hand and gently

181

patted the other's glistening dome, and Norbert cringed as if he had expected a punch.

'I hope so, Professor,' said the Saint softly. 'You see, I have this dislike for characters who try to murder me. And I'm not much fonder of people who'd let me have a nasty accident without making any attempt to help me. I'd hate to think that of you, Louis.'

Once again Norbert began to babble his protestations of innocence and good intention, but Simon stopped him.

'You said the police wanted to see us. Well, we had better not keep the good gendarmes waiting.'

With Norbert in tow he cut across the lawn towards the house. Down by the outbuildings a uniformed man was talking to some workers, and he saw that an ambulance had arrived at the *chai* and a stretcher was being slid into it.

'Where?' asked the Saint as they entered the château and Norbert mumbled, 'The salon.'

The gendarme leaning against the wall outside the salon eyed them disinterestedly as they approached from the main hall. As they drew closer he reluctantly levered himself upright and opened the door. The opening let out Philippe Florian's indignant voice:

'I object to being questioned as if we had something to hide. I shall . . .'

The protest tailed off as Philippe realised that he had lost the attention of his audience. The

182

Saint took one step into the room and paused to survey the scene. It made him think of a still displayed outside a cinema.

Yves was standing in front of the fireplace with his hands clasped behind his back. Philippe and Mimette sat at opposite ends of the sofa while Henri stood by the window. Jeanne Corday was lounging with practised poise against the wall beside her fiancé, watching the spiralling smoke from her cigarette with affected boredom.

'So good of you to join us,' said Philippe.

'You make me feel like one of the family,' the Saint replied sweetly.

He strolled composedly across to the collection of bottles and glasses on a side table. Jeanne's welcome was warmer. She smiled and almost mouthed a kiss as he passed, and the Saint winked back. Henri scowled at both of them.

'Simon, where have you been?' asked Mimette, with puzzled concern in her voice.

He glanced down at himself, and tried to dust off some of the traces of his desperate scramble back to the battlements before pouring himself a stiff measure of malt and perching himself on the edge of the table.

'Just hanging about,' he said lightly. 'And where is the local Lecoq? Gone home already, or is he disguised as that sentry at the door?'

'Sergeant Olivet wanted to see my uncle's

183

cottage. Charles has taken him,' supplied Henri.

The Saint looked enquiringly at Mimette, and the slight shake of her head told him that their visit had not been discussed.

'Exactly where have you been, Monsieur Templar?' Yves asked temperately. 'Surely you knew the police would want to see you?'

The Saint smiled.

'The police always want to see me. Actually I went to the tower to admire the view, only I nearly became part of it.'

In clipped undramatic sentences he outlined what had happened.

'The professor was on his way to tell you the good news, but unfortunately I spoiled his moment of glory,' he concluded.

Norbert had stayed by the door but he still could not avoid the Saint's searching gaze. He squirmed uncomfortably in the focus of the eyes turned towards him.

'A shocking accident—a miraculous escape,' he mumbled. 'Really, there should be signs warning people away from some parts of these ancient buildings.'

'Oh Simon! You could have been killed,' breathed Mimette.

The Saint shrugged deprecatingly. The incident was already fading from his mind, crowded out by more immediate concerns. Risks were part and parcel of his vocation, and he dismissed them as quickly as most men

184

would have forgotten a slight slip on an icy sidewalk.

'What sort of cop is this Sergeant Olivet?' he asked, when the subject of his escape from a squishy death had been briefly exhausted.

'Olivet? He seems efficient enough,' answered Yves neutrally.

Mimette was more forthcoming.

'He is ambitious, I think. I've talked to him several times, he has always come himself when we have had any trouble. The last time was just after the fire at the barn.'

Philippe looked at his watch and asked irritably: 'What's keeping the damn man? Does he expect us to sit around here all night?'

Almost as if he had been waiting for his cue, the door opened to admit the subject of Philippe's annoyance.

He was small for a policeman, scarcely average height, and his khaki uniform was cut to a degree of perfection rarely attained by police tailors. His hair, which was meticulously trimmed, was as black and shiny as his shoes, and the sheen of his belt and the brightness of the buckle would have won applause from any sergeant-major. His face was tanned and smooth but saved from being bland by a pair of piercing black eyes that darted continuously from person to person.

A couple of paces behind the sergeant came Charles and after him the gendarme from the hall, who no longer appeared lethargic as he closed the door and placed himself in front of it, his hand resting on the holster on his belt.

Olivet nodded to Yves but walked towards the Saint. In his left hand he carried his pillbox cap and in his right a small package wrapped in sacking. He placed both carefully on the table before addressing the Saint.

'Monsieur Simon Templar, I am Sergeant Olivet. I am here to make preliminary enquiries into the murder of Gaston Pichot.'

His tone was quiet but authoritative, and he appeared very conscious that he was the centre of interest and clearly intended to keep matters that way.

'Good for you,' Simon drawled, sipping his drink.

'I was surprised when I was told that you were a guest at Ingare,' Olivet continued. 'It is not the sort of place where one expects to meet the famous Simon Templar.'

'Oh, I get around to the most respectable places,' the Saint replied coolly.

'It is interesting, though,' Olivet mused, and seemed to be talking more to himself than to anyone else, 'that a Templar should go out of his way to visit a place once so closely associated with the *Templiers*. Almost too extraordinary a coincidence, one might say.'

'You might, but I wouldn't,' the Saint countered. The interview was developing into a verbal fencing match with more hazards then he had anticipated. He had only expected to answer the normal when, where, why, and how type of questions that he was used to being asked in such circumstances.

'Until I came here,' he said, 'you could have written everything I knew about the Templars on a postcard and still had room for the stamp. I was driving from Avignon, heading for the Riviera. I picked up a couple of hitch-hikers and gave them a lift here. When we arrived, a couple of hoodlums were setting fire to the barn. I did what I could to help, and Mademoiselle Florian kindly invited me to stay when my car broke down. It's as simple as that.'

Olivet's eyes stopped their perpetual motion and bored into the Saint.

'The car that the arsonists used was stolen from Avignon that morning,' he said at last. 'It is interesting that you were also in Avignon at the time.'

'Me and a few thousand others. So the idea is that I hired a couple of *voyous* to burn down the barn, picked up a pair of hitch-hikers as a cover, and arranged to arrive on the scene in the nick of time to prove myself a hero.'

Olivet appeared to consider the possibility.

'It would have been an ingenious plan to ingratiate yourself, worthy of the famous Saint.'

The famous Saint sighed.

'Or a brilliant theory that might get a

187

gendarme promoted? Unfortunately his superiors might have just enough brains to think he'd been out too long in the hot sun.'

Olivet flushed. He said coldly: 'I have heard about your attitude to authority, Monsieur Templar. I advise you not to try such tactics with me.'

'And I advise you to stop trying to dream up ridiculous theories and get on with finding Gaston's murderer. If you want my help you can have it.'

'Help?' Olivet rolled the word meditatively. 'Perhaps you can help to identify this.'

Carefully he undid the package he had brought in, to reveal a short poker. It was about ten inches long and topped with an elaborately tooled brass handle. Holding it delicately in a fold of its erstwhile wrapping, he held it up like an exhibit.

The Saint's eyes narrowed as he inspected it. He needed no one to tell him the origin of the red stickiness on the end of the shaft.

Olivet turned so that the others in the room could see it.

'This was found in Gaston Pichot's cottage. I believe it to be the murder weapon.'

Mimette looked quickly away, but for the others it appeared to hold a morbid fascination. Olivet returned his attention to the Saint.

'Do you recognise it?'

'Don't tell me, let me guess. It's a poker.'

188

Olivet tensed at the Saint's flippancy, and his voice took on a harder edge.

'A rather fine one. You see the handle carries the Florian crest encircled by a large spray of daffodils as the base of the motif.'

'Very pretty,' Simon observed impassively. 'So what?'

'It seems too good to have been owned by the murdered man, yet it was found in his cottage. How would you explain that?'

'Perhaps the murderer took it with him. I'm told that people who intend to put out other people's lights quite often like the reassurance of knowing they have the required blunt instrument in hand,' the Saint replied.

Olivet seemed delighted with the suggestion. The Saint decided that if he ever left the *gendarmerie* he would be a cinch on the stage. He was certainly making a great build-up to his dramatic moment—whatever that was to be.

Olivet turned to Charles, who had been standing near the door with the attentive self-effacement of the perfectly trained servant.

'I believe you recognised it?' he said, and the major-domo nodded slowly.

'It is one of a set.'

'And how many sets like this are there in the château?'

'Only one exactly like that. The crest is on all of them, but the flowers differ according to the room the set was made for.'

Olivet paused theatrically before delivering his apocalyptic question: 'And where is this set kept?'

'The servant looked directly at the Saint for the first time, and Simon could see the accusing bitterness in his eyes.

'In the room of Monsieur Templar.'

2

Simon Templar made no effort to hide the shock and astonishment that jolted him.

He had not really studied the chasing on the poker's handle when Olivet displayed it, and even the mention of daffodils had not immediately rung a bell. The symbolic painting on the door of his guest room, and Charles's explanation of it, were far enough in the past, and far enough removed in context from Gaston's death and the present situation, for Olivet's bombshell to catch him completely off his guard.

At that moment, to a shrewd analyst, the very transparency of his reaction might have been the most convincing evidence of his innocence. But the Saint knew at once that he could not count on that kind of shrewdness. As he looked around the room and watched the significance of the old retainer's words registering, he realised that it was going to take all his resourcefulness to ride this one out.

It was not utterly astounding that the

murderer had attempted to frame him: he was after all the ideal candidate. What took him aback was the manner in which the frame had been so subtly thought out and cold-bloodedly accomplished. After the amateurish ransacking of Gaston's cottage, he had not credited the murderer with the degree of finesse that had just been demonstrated.

In the cold light of a court room, any competent advocate would have shown Olivet's find to be blatantly circumstantial. But in the charged atmosphere of Ingare, the Saint was acutely aware that it would take some fast talking for him to remain on the scene long enough to discover the person responsible.

The silence was growing more tense with every second that crawled past, until the dropping of the proverbial pin would have sounded like the detonation of a mine. The Saint seized the initiative by being the one who broke it.

'Well, leaving a great clumsy clue like that doesn't seem to me like the famous Simon Templar,' he remarked, recovering his nonchalance. 'I hope it doesn't make you think silly thoughts about me, Sergeant. I wouldn't be in too much of a hurry to bring out the bracelets and wait for the medal if I were you.'

'I don't think the bracelets, as you call them, would be necessary,' retorted Olivet suavely, and Simon saw the gendarme at the door flip open the top of his holster and rest his hand on the butt of his pistol.

'You can't be seriously thinking of arresting me?' said the Saint with the utmost incredulity.

'*Pas encore, peut-être,*' Olivet said, with deliberate emphasis on the second word.

Philippe banged his glass down on the arm of the sofa with a force that sent the liquid inside slopping over the rim.

'Why not?' he bellowed. 'If he is a well known criminal—'

Olivet turned to him and spoke sharply.

'Monsieur Florian, you will kindly let me carry out this investigation in my own way.'

'What the Sergeant means,' Simon explained, in the tone a teacher might use to a particularly slow-witted child, 'is that he is not yet sure enough of his evidence. And he doesn't want to end up looking a fool. One fool is enough for any party.'

Philippe pointed to the poker that Olivet still held.

'Not sure of his evidence?' he repeated scornfully. 'What do you call that?'

'I call that a frame. What do you call it?' the Saint returned evenly, and before Philippe could renew his protest turned to Charles. 'Are the guest rooms in this house locked up when the guests are out?'

The major-domo looked uncertainly at Olivet, and waited until the sergeant indicated that he should answer the question before replying that they were not.

'And there is only yourself and your wife to look after them?'

'*Oui.*'

'Which means,' Simon continued, turning back to Olivet, 'that anyone, including the estimable Charles himself, at almost any time, could have lifted the poker with hardly any risk of being seen.'

'And yet you yourself never noticed that it was missing!'

'Why should I? There's been no need for a fire lately. More to the point, Charles did not miss it, or is not admitting if he did. And if I had left it at Gaston's, I could certainly have retrieved it when I went there earlier this evening.'

Olivet was momentarily startled out of the complacent attitude he had adopted.

'You went there? Why?'

'Because when I helped to lift Gaston's body out of the vat, I could tell that he had been dead for at least six hours. He had been recovering from a fall, resting at the cottage. So that seemed a likely place for him to have been murdered. While we were waiting for you to arrive, Mademoiselle Mimette and I went there to have a look.'

'You did not mention this, Mademoiselle,' said Olivet suspiciously.

193

'I must have forgotten,' she said carelessly.

With a frown, the gendarme turned again to the Saint, inviting him to go on.

'When we got there, the place had been ransacked. The poker may have been there, but as everything was in such a mess I thought it best to leave it as it was until you had seen it. If I'd been stupid enough to leave a murder weapon behind, I could easily have removed it then. But I wasn't even looking for blunt instruments at the time.'

The Saint saw Philippe start.

'Ransacked? But Gaston had nothing worth stealing.'

'That's what I thought—but how do you know?' the Saint enquired, and Philippe suddenly found himself again the centre of attention.

'I don't,' he said quickly. 'But Gaston was only a foreman. How could he have had anything worth killing for?'

'Somebody obviously thought he had,' the Saint pointed out. 'I wonder if they found it.'

Olivet was beginning to look uncomfortable. The aura of confident authority that had surrounded him a few minutes earlier was rapidly dissolving. He spoke cautiously, weighing his words.

'I think the rest of this interview should be conducted at the *gendarmerie*.'

The Saint smiled. To certain other detectives

in other spots of the globe that smile in itself would have been sufficient warning that the battle they thought they had won was really just beginning.

'The only way I go there with you is if you arrest me,' he said coolly. 'And you're not going to arrest me because there are so many holes in your so-called evidence that you could use it for a colander.'

Olivet was not accustomed to having his invitations so calmly declined, but he recovered quickly.

'Perhaps you do not understand, Monsieur Templar, that in France it is you who are required to prove yourself innocent, not the police who must prove you guilty.'

'I know all about the *Code Napoléon*,' Simon said imperturbably. 'But you still have to present some sort of case, and you don't have one that would last five minutes in court.'

Olivet fidgeted beneath the ice-blue gaze that was focused on him. When the Saint continued, he was addressing the sergeant for the benefit of everyone present.

'Let's look at this so-called evidence. You have a murder weapon, lucky you. It's from my room, unlucky me. But that's as far as it goes. You haven't yet had time to test it for fingerprints. You don't have a professional opinion about when Gaston was killed, so you don't know whether I have an alibi or not. You don't even know why he was murdered. In fact the sum total of what you don't know is staggering.'

Simon paused for a moment, to make his counterpoint more telling.

'What you do know is that if you arrest me tonight, it'll be front page news in every paper in Europe tomorrow, and in a few hours there'll be more reporters around here than vines. You'll be the big hero for a day. The cop who finally sewed up the Saint. But you also know that if you don't make it stick you'll be the laughing stock of every police force from Paris to Pago-Pago, and afterwards you'll be lucky if your bosses trust you to look for lost dogs.'

For effective punctuation, the Saint took another unhurried sip from his glass. He went on with nerveless precision, taking aim and scoring like a marksman:

'When you stop being dazzled with dreams of glory, you know damn well that I wouldn't have my reputation if I went about murdering people and leaving clues that a blind man couldn't help tripping over. The only thing we know for sure is that the killer was someone who is free to go anywhere in the château—which isn't just me.'

It was an effective enough speech in its own way, he decided, even if it didn't reach the heights attained in some similar confrontations in the past. But the mixture of contempt and logic was still volatile enough to have had Chief

196

Inspector Claud Eustace Teal groping for another soothing strip of Wrigley's or Inspector John Fernack yearning for the freedom of a downtown backroom and a length of rubber hose.

However, the Saint knew the kind of ground he was on. The averagely ignorant foreigner, if he thinks about such matters at all, thinks of all French law officers as 'gendarmes', whereas in fact the gendarmes are the rural constabulary, who operate outside the metropolitan districts which have their own police forces, whose officers are correctly called *agents*. It was Simon Templar's business to know things like that; he knew that he was not dealing with a really sophisticated top cop, nor would any such phenomenon materialise to take charge in the instant future. A case at Ingare would have to percolate up through enough echelons of bureaucracy to give time for quite a few developments before it came into summit jurisdiction.

Olivet looked distinctly unhappy. His black eyes probed the Saint uncertainly. As a rural policeman, not a big city detective, he was not used to prospective prisoners arguing so eloquently and adumbrating pictures of potential disaster that infiltrated his stomach with butterflies.

Philippe was less impressed.

'He's bluffing,' he told Olivet. 'If he isn't the

197

killer, it would have to be one of us. Which is absurd.'

Simon cocked a sardonic eyebrow.

'How comforting for you,' he murmured.

The sergeant tried to reassert the authority of his office.

'As I have already said, Monsieur Florian, this is only a preliminary enquiry. I am here to make a report on which the Department will act, and that is all.'

'And I apologise to Monsieur Templar,' said Mimette, 'for any attempt to make him our scapegoat.'

Yves Florian looked intently into the Saint's face as if seeking some form of reassurance. Finally he said: 'Monsieur Templar has helped us a great deal since he arrived here, and I personally have confidence in him. If it would be any help, he can remain here as my guest until your investigations are completed.'

'*Et en voilà pour la solidarité de la famille*,' said Philippe scathingly.

Olivet was plainly undecided, although Yves's offer had made a deep impression on him. And then, to the Saint's surprise, Henri came in on his side.

'I think that offer should be accepted,' he told the sergeant, and continued in the same flat unemotional tone as if addressing a tribunal. 'As a lawyer, I must agree with Monsieur Templar that you have insufficient grounds on which to

198

arrest him, certainly not enough to even contemplate going to court. Therefore if he gave an undertaking to remain available for questioning, there need be no sensational publicity. You have said that he is well known; surely that is the one reason why he is unlikely to run away. He would be caught within hours.'

The Saint kept a straight face as he remembered the days when half the police forces of Europe had hunted him across the continent without success, but he did not feel it politic to air his reminiscences at that moment.

Henri added: 'I was very fond of my uncle. I want to see his murderer caught. But I also know that he would not have wished the family to be subjected to the publicity that will surely result if Monsieur Templar is arrested.'

Olivet was visibly relieved. He avoided looking at Philippe and spoke directly to Yves.

'*Eh bien*—we shall continue when I have fingerprints and a medical report. Meanwhile, I shall expect all of you to be at my disposition here.'

'But you can't leave us like that,' protested Norbert. 'None of us will be safe. We still have a murderer in the château!'

'Then you will be most anxious to find him,' Olivet said maliciously. 'I don't think you have anything to fear for the moment, but I shall leave a man here in case.'

Carefully he rewrapped the poker and picked

up his *képi*. The gendarme at the door fastened his holster and returned to his former pose of stolid indifference. The sergeant bowed himself out with a curtly formal '*A beintôt, messieurs-dames.*'

Understandably, the dinner that Charles served soon afterwards, with impeccable frigidity, was far from convivial. The tension across the table was almost tangible. Jeanne and Henri sat in a frosted silence which showed that their quarrel of the afternoon had not been made up. In addition Henri was subjected to a cold shoulder from his employer that must have had him wondering where his next pay cheque was coming from. Norbert stayed as far away from the Saint as the confines of the room allowed, and hurriedly excused himself as soon as the cheese was served. Only Yves and Mimette made a brave pretence of table talk, and that was clearly at the dictation of good manners.

Mimette made one forlorn attempt to lighten the general pall of gloom.

'Sitting here like so many zombies won't bring Gaston back,' she said. 'And I don't think he would have wanted to be remembered this way.'

'It is hardly amusing,' Philippe said heavily, 'to think that even a Florian could be accused of his murder, if suspicion is not confined to others.'

'*Sans doute,*' retorted Mimette, 'every

murderer's family has always felt the same, when one of them turned out to be a bad egg.'

'That is still only a theory from a *roman policier*,' Yves intervened soothingly. 'There may be some other explanation altogether. Until we know, we do not have to think we are all criminals.'

It was an argument that seemed to make little impression. Minutes after the service of coffee, Simon found himself left in the small salon alone with Mimette, who had declined Yves's discreet offer to see her to her room.

'I'm flattered,' said the Saint, after the door had closed, 'that you aren't terrified to be left at the mercy of a well-known outlaw.'

'*Evidemment, je suis idiote*,' she said, looking straight at him, 'but I would trust you more than anyone here, except my own father.'

He took the liberty of replenishing his snifter of Armagnac.

'What I'd like to know,' he said, 'is why Philippe wants me in the Bastille.'

'Isn't it obvious?' said Mimette bitterly.

He shook his head.

'It's too obvious. That's what worries me. Naturally if he killed Gaston, he'd be specially keen to see the murder pinned on me. But however you feel about your uncle, you can't think he's stupid. I can't see him being so unsubtle as to make everyone think what you're thinking.'

'Well, what else would turn him so much against you?'

Simon paced across the room and back, scowling at the inoffensive walls. His answers themselves came out as questions.

'Because to him the most important thing is to get the whole scandal swept under the carpet? To get anyone arrested who isn't part of the Florian household? Because I'm the most suspectable outsider?... Or because he has quite another guilty secret, which he's afraid I might stumble on if I'm allowed to stay around here and play detective?... How nice it would be to be a mind-reader!'

He subsided on to the settee beside her. He was exasperated by the passive role that had been thrust upon him, by having to expand theories while waiting for something else to happen, when his own instinct had always been for positive action. But what action was possible?

He wished, suddenly, that he could have found himself there at Ingare with no mystery to cloud the pleasure of discovering his possible remote link with its ancient history—and its present beautiful descendant.

They sat listening to the lulling whisper of the wind through the ivy and watching the moon lay a shifting golden path across the lawn. The breeze carried the subtle smells of the countryside to freshen and clear heads blocked by half-truths and unanswered questions. A few wisps of grey drifted lazily across a sky of purple and diamonds. It was a night created for making love, not thinking about murder or sifting the secrets of the long dead.

Mimette sighed deeply, and the Saint put his arm around her shoulders and drew her closer.

'Simon, when will it end?' she whispered, and he stroked her hair with gently caressing fingers and did not reply at once.

'I wish I knew,' he said at length. 'But it can't be long.'

His hands traced the delicate outline of her profile. He had never seen her look more exciting or more vulnerable. He looked into her eyes and saw stirring in their depths a longing and a frightened urgency that he had never seen before, a plea that he was incapable of refusing.

Her mouth parted at the touch of his lips, and it was a long time before either of them returned to an awareness of their surroundings.

3

Simon Templar's career made many tiresome demands of him, and as he finished breakfast the following morning he was presented with one of them. He was enjoying his second cup of coffee by the time the rest of the household began to wander downstairs in search of their first.

Mimette was the first to appear. She looked at

him uncertainly for a moment. She studiously busied herself with her food, masking any embarrassment with a screen of small talk.

As the Saint had hoped, Yves was the next to enter the dining-room. He held out his hand to greet Simon with the utmost cordiality.

'*Bonjour, Monsieur Templar. Vous avez bien dormi?*'

It is an immutable tenet of French good manners, often baffling to strangers, that a guest must be greeted every day with a handshake and a query as to whether he slept well. The Saint responded punctiliously, and then came straight to the matter that had brought him out of his bed so early.

'I need to go into Carpentras this morning to see about my car. Have you a car I could borrow?'

Yves regarded him hesitantly, his confidence in his guest wrestling with inevitable suspicion. It was patently an excuse rather than a reason, but he did not ask why the Saint could not simply telephone the garage. Perhaps it was politeness, or more likely because he was just too tired to care.

Philippe, who had arrived just in time to hear the request, had no such inhibition.

'I thought we had all given our word to be at Olivet's disposition here,' he said.

'I shall be, whenever he wants me,' Simon replied calmly. 'I'm not planning to run away.

In fact, you'd have to kick me out bodily to get rid of me now, before the great Ingare mystery has been solved.'

Almost as if apologising for his earlier doubts, Yves said: 'Yes, of course, you can take my car.'

'But today is the meeting of the *Confrérie Vinicole*,' Mimette reminded him.

Yves shrugged his shoulders apathetically.

'What does it matter? They can do without me for one week. They will have heard about what has happened. I don't want to listen to their gossip and answer their questions.'

'But you always go,' Mimette insisted. 'He can take my car.'

Yves looked at his daughter with weary eyes. He sat hunched over the table, idly stirring his untasted coffee as if even the task of lifting the cup would require an effort he no longer possessed.

'What use is the *Confrérie* when there is no *vin*?' he asked wryly.

'I don't understand,' said Mimette.

'Don't you?' Yves sighed. 'It is really very simple. We needed a good harvest this year—'

'And we had one.'

'Yes, Mimette. But Gaston's murder...' Yves shivered. 'When the news is reported—'

'What your father means,' Philippe said, quite brutally, 'is that when it becomes known that bodies are found floating in vats at Château Ingare, nobody is going to rush out and buy our

205

wine, however much of it there is or however good it may be.'

'I'm afraid you must expect the headlines,' said the Saint more gently. 'It's the sort of story news editors dream about. FAITHFUL RETAINER FOUND DEAD IN CHATEAU RIDDLE, etcetera. That's why the murderer went to all the trouble of moving Gaston's body from the cottage. Whoever wants you out is prepared to go to any lengths to help you on your way.'

'But I thought that Gaston was killed because—'

'Yes, of course,' Simon interrupted quickly. The last thing he wanted at that moment was to involve Yves in speculations about the treasure. 'But somebody also saw it as an opportunity to hurt the business, and he made the most of it.'

'And it is more important for me to be thinking how we are going to cope with that, than to attend a luncheon meeting of the *Confrérie*,' Yves concluded. 'So, Mimette, when you have finished, will you please show Monsieur Templar where to find my car.'

'*Merci infiniment*,' said the Saint sincerely. 'I shall try to take good care of it.'

When he left the dining-room with Mimette soon afterwards, the gendarme whom Olivet had left as a watchdog was standing in the hall, looking very official and determined, if perhaps a little vague as to what he was supposed to be determined about.

Not knowing what the gendarme's instructions might be, Simon gave him a cheerful and confident good day, and added, while giving Mimette's arm a warning squeeze: 'Monsieur Florian will see you as soon as he has finished breakfast.'

They went on out to the forecourt, and the man made no move to detain or follow them.

Mimette guided the Saint around the house to where a stable block had been converted into a row of garages. She unlocked the one at the far end, and he helped her to drag back the double doors. His eyes widened in amazement and delight at the gleaming white Mercedes inside.

'A German car?'

Mimette smiled.

'It was the staff car of the local Commandant. When the soldiers pulled out it was left behind, and my father kept it as part payment for their use of the château.'

It was a late 30's model, a four-door open limousine of majestic proportions with the rear seat raised to add to the stature and prestige of its former owner.

Simon slid behind the wheel and was silent for a few minutes while he familiarised himself with the controls. He started the engine and rolled the big car out into the courtyard.

'Why couldn't you just phone the garage?' Mimette asked suddenly.

The Saint shook his head.

'The Hirondel is like my baby. I want to see for myself what they're doing to it.'

'When will you be back?'

'Some time after lunch,' he said. 'I promise.'

She stepped aside and he let in the clutch again. The Mercedes leapt forward, and he spun the wheel and accelerated, to disappear through the gateway of the courtyard with an impudent squeal of rubber which from any ordinary driver would have raised doubts about the seriousness of his pledge to treat the car with great care.

Despite its age, the Merc handled magnificently and had obviously been meticulously maintained. The Saint settled back into the soft leather of the seat and revelled in the feel of the rushing wind on his face. His hands caressed the wheel as he steered the car out of the lane which served the château on to the main road and turned the gunsight radiator emblem towards Carpentras.

He allowed the problems of the Florians to fade temporarily from his mind as the château was reduced to a miniature on the hilltop behind and then disappeared completely. He felt glad to be away from the tension for a while, and gave himself up wholeheartedly to enjoying the drive.

Gradually the vine-covered slopes were left behind, to be replaced by small fruit farms and market gardens. In the distance, the sharply sculptured peaks of the Dentelles de Montmirail made a picture in the rear-view mirror. He drove at speed not because he was in any hurry to reach the town but simply for the pleasure it gave him and the exhilarating sensation of freedom that pumped from the engine's eight cylinders.

Simon Templar's life had been saved in many strange ways and by a weird assortment of people whom his ever-watchful guardian angel had caused to be in the right place at the appointed time; but never before had he had cause to thank a cat. He was passing a small row of cottages on the outskirts of Aubignan when the animal darted across his path in a blur of black and white fur that had him stamping on the brake instinctively. His foot drove the pedal to the floor, but the speedometer needle only registered the effect of taking his foot off the accelerator.

He swung the wheel, deducting one of the animal's nine lives, and pulled on the handbrake. The lever rose with sickening ease and the car continued to hurtle on.

The Saint crashed down through the gears with a violence that had the engine screaming in protest, but the braking result was then too late for any possibility of taking the sharp curve that loomed suddenly ahead, with a tidily spaced border of shade trees ruling out any chance of shunting on to soft shoulder.

In a matter of micro-seconds, his brain

worked out equations of distance, speed, and centrifugal force. Like a galvanised jack-in-the-box, he jumped from his seat on to the door, braced a foot against the windshield pillar, and launched himself out and backwards, giving the maximum neutralisation to his inherent momentum. If he got it right, he should be able to hit a gap between the tree trunks.

4

He landed with legs flexing to take the first shock, and rolled like a parachutist. His left arm and shoulder curled into the impact, and the reflex action that relaxed the rest of his body saved him from injury as he somersaulted across the verge and cannoned into the base of the hedge beyond. As he finally came to rest, he heard the sickening crunch of tortured metal and shattering glass which told him that the car too had finished its journey.

He lay still for a moment while he regained his breath and then climbed to his feet and walked towards the wreck.

The Mercedes lay upside down beside the road. His final spin of the wheel had caused it to skid off the bend, and it had hit a tree broadside on, rebounded, and overturned. One rear wheel was still forlornly turning as he reached it.

The offside wing had been all but ripped away, and the rest of that coachwork stove in. The headlights, front fender, and most of the

210

other external attachments had been torn off. The Saint snaked a hand under the dashboard and killed the engine. The air was heavy with the stench of petrol, and he was surprised that the tank had not exploded on impact. The steering column was embedded in the back of the driver's seat, and he did not care to dwell on what his fate would have been if he had stayed there.

He breathed silent thanks to the impetuous feline whose sudden appearance had saved him. If he had not been forced to brake as sharply when he did, he would have drifted into the corner at full speed and by then it would have been of purely academic interest. He thought back over the drive and realised that it was only because of the negligible traffic that the braking systems had not been put under pressure before.

One brake failure may be an accident, two brakes failing simultaneously is almost certainly attempted murder. Simon did not bother to investigate the wreckage to prove his hypothesis but scanned the surrounding terrain for signs of a telephone or transport.

His predicament was so obvious that the first truck that came along stopped at once. Fortunately the driver's home base was Carpentras, and he sympathetically took the Saint all the way to the garage he had set out to look for.

The Hirondel stood in a bay next to the

entrance, where passers-by could not fail to notice it, as proof of the quality of the establishment's clientèle. The paintwork had been waxed until it blazed and the light sparkled along the recently polished chrome trimmings. It shamed the production-line boxes around it like a peacock amid a flock of barnyard hens. He glanced inside at the dashboard but bore no grudge when the tripmeter showed that it had already been given a lengthy and unauthorised road test.

He was starting to open the front to check the radiator when a voice behind him suggested forcefully that he should desist and depart. The words chosen to convey the message have no place in a narrative that may be read by minors, maiden aunts, or deacons of the Faith. The Saint turned, and the unfriendly expression on the mechanic's grease-smeared countenance turned to one of welcome and contrition. He offered a thousand apologies for not having recognised the Saint, and Simon accepted one.

'Is she ready?' he asked.

The mechanic beamed.

'What a beautiful car!'

Simon smiled tolerantly.

'Yes, I know, but is she ready?'

The mechanic admitted that she was, and went on to explain how in addition to replacing the radiator he had tuned the carburettor, balanced the wheels, repaired a small hole in the silencer of which the Saint was unaware, and given the entire vehicle a complete lubrication.

'Now I have another job for you,' said the Saint, when the *garagiste* had finished the account of his labours.

He recited the essentials of his accident and gave its location.

'Bring it in as soon as you can and see if it's good for anything but the scrap-heap. I'll be back for the bad news after lunch.'

He asked directions for the post office, which had always been his second destination. It was near the centre of the old town, facing the Palais de Justice across the pleasant open square in front of the five-hundred-year-old cathedral of St. Siffrein. He wrote the Paris phone number he wanted on a slip of paper and handed it in at the counter. It was, he reflected, a roundabout way to make a simple telephone call, but the chances of being overheard at the château had left him no choice, and it was actually the main reason for his trip to Carpentras.

He had absorbed most of the information on the official notices that lined the walls by the time the clerk announced that his call was ready and he went into one of the booths to take it. He heard the operator check the number, and then the gentle voice that brought the memories of a darker and more violent era flooding back.

'Do you still stock the works of François Villon?' the Saint enquired, and smiled to

213

himself as he pictured Antoine Louvois in his small bookshop near the Odéon reacting to that simple question.

He could see the tall greying figure, the keen alert eyes, and the slender hands that held the receiver. And he remembered another day when those same artistic hands had grasped the plunger of a detonator and instantly sent a score of Nazis into the heaven of the Herrenvolk.

There was an appreciable pause before the answer he was expecting crackled along the line.

'We do not have much demand for those old works today.'

'*Mais où sont les neiges d'antan?*' sighed the Saint.

There was another pause before the other requested him to repeat his words.

'But where are the snows of yesteryear?' Simon quoted again, and laughed softly. 'Do you forget so easily?'

'Simon! Where are you?'

'In Provence, in Carpentras, and it would take too long to explain why, but I'm going to bother you again.'

'It is so good to hear from you. You are coming to Paris?'

'Not right now, Antoine. But I need some information and you may be able to help me.'

'*Tu n'as qu'à demander, cher ami.*'

'I want you to think back to the war, to the Occupation. Does the name Florian mean

214

anything to you? Philippe Florian?'

Again there was a pause and the Saint added: 'Dark, stockily built, about forty-five. Apparently had links with the black market in Paris.'

Louvois chuckled.

'Ah, you mean *Le Caméléon*.'

The soubriquet seemed particularly inappropriate. Somehow the Saint could not imagine the portly figure of Philippe Florian merging into any background, but he remembered that members of the Resistance had used many strange nicknames to protect themselves. Louvois himself had been known as Colonel Eglantine.

'*Alors?*' Simon prompted.

'A brave and useful man,' said Louvois seriously. 'He was big in the black market, it is true, but that was a good cover. The Germans thought he was a collaborator, so they tolerated his activities, but the information he gained he passed on to the Resistance. His connections helped us in many ways.'

'Then why did he run when the Allies took Paris?'

'He was in the middle. Not many people knew of his work. He had to go to ground until his name was cleared. Only a few collaborators ever got to trial,' Louvois added pointedly.

'You don't know anything about what he has been doing since the war ended, I suppose,' asked the Saint hopefully.

'A wealthy man, I believe,' Louvois replied. 'I think he has several successful businesses, but I could find out more if you like.'

'I'd be very grateful. Can I phone you again after lunch? Also anything on his assistant, Henri Pichot.'

'*Bien volontiers*. I will see what I can do.'

The Saint emerged from the gloom of the post office and went in search of sustenance. A stroll down the Rue de la République brought him to the only restaurant listed in his edition of the Guide Michelin, the Univers, a modest but comfortable hostelry overlooking the Place Aristide Briand, on the perimeter of the old town. He enjoyed an eminently satisfying meal of *pâté maison* followed by a robustly garlicked preparation of tripes for which he had an uninhibited affection, but in the interests of dental hygiene eschewed a toffee-flavoured dessert which paid tribute to the town's traditional product. He lingered over the bottle of ice-cold *rosé* which he had ordered at the beginning of the repast, before estimating that it was not too soon for a leisured return to the Place d'Inguimbert and his second call to Antoine Louvois.

Again he wrote down the number and waited until the clerk announced that despite the efforts of the French telephone system his call had been connected.

'Any luck?' Simon asked as soon as he was put through.

This time he did not have to identify himself.

'A little,' Louvois replied guardedly. 'Florian owns a couple of factories, light engineering. He started after the war with a small Government contract and never looked back. Recently bought into a chain of American-style snack bars. They're doing well too.'

'*Quelle horreur!*' said the Saint with feeling. 'But does anything shady seem to be involved?'

'Nothing you could be definite about. There was talk that his Government contracts were payment for something someone didn't want made public, probably to do with the war. And I'm told that some of his financial dealings have been pretty close to the borderline. He got into the snack business after a couple of fires almost bankrupted the company. There is always gossip when things like that happen.'

'And Pichot?'

'Apparently he handles the legal side for Florian. Very sharp and very ambitious, so I'm told. Lives well, too. An apartment near the Etiole, likes his nights out in the best places, and has *petite amie* with expensive tastes.'

The Saint thought of Jeanne Corday and smiled.

'Thanks, that's enough for now. Antoine, you have been a great help.'

'Are you in trouble, Simon?'

217

Simon laughed.

'Nothing I can't handle, *mon pôte*. Next time I'm in Paris I'll tell you all about it.'

'I shall look forward to it.

'*Moi aussi.*'

He walked back to the garage with a new lightness in his step. The information he had gleaned was nothing substantial but it had been just enough to brush away the cobwebs of some theories that had hampered him. He was in no hurry to return to Ingare. His next move was already decided upon, and that was not scheduled until later in the day.

The Mercedes was in the workshop, a pathetically crumpled appendage to the crane on the breakdown truck. After a long silent survey, the Saint was able to make his own painful prognosis.

'Maybe we could sell it to some art gallery as a piece of modern sculpture,' he said.

'It could perhaps be completely rebuilt,' the *garagiste* told him hopefully.

'You had better keep it until Monsieur Florian decides what is to be done with it,' said the Saint.

He paid his bill and added a generous tip, and pointed the Hirondel back towards Château Ingare.

His return journey was undertaken at a conservative pace, and the first shades of evening were spreading across the hillside by the time he retraced the rough road by which he had first entered the *domaine*. A group of workmen were standing talking beside the burned-out barn, but as the Saint passed their conversation ceased abruptly, and they watched him in sullen silence as he drove on the the château.

Mimette was talking to the watchdog gendarme at the top of the steps outside the front door as Simon braked to a halt, which happily solved a couple of potential problems. She smoothly suppressed any visible surprise at his return in a different car, as if in any case his day-long absence was nothing remarkable, and went in with him through the hall to the salon.

Only there did she say: 'You have a lot to tell me.'

The Saint helped himself to a Scotch of the generous proportions that he felt his day had earned him.

'It's going to be a bit harder,' he said, 'to tell your father about his precious Merc.'

As he undramatically related the day's events, the revelation of Philippe's wartime activities shook her only slightly less than the sabotaging of the car.

'You could have been killed,' she said.

'I almost was. And your father certainly would have been.'

'You saved his life.'

'*Pas du tout*. I wrecked his car.'

She bowed her head with a barely perceptible

219

shudder.

'It doesn't make sense,' she said at last. 'Why should anyone want to kill my father?'

'No Yves, no Ingare,' Simon answered succinctly. 'Whoever did it knew that your father always went to that *Confrérie* lunch on the same day every week. The fact that he didn't go today, and I borrowed the car, was unfortunate—for them.'

'And Philippe, why did he not tell his own family what he had done? Why did he allow us to think he was a collaborator?'

'Perhaps you never gave him the chance,' suggested the Saint. 'I'm not as surprised as you. The way he helped me get Gaston out of the vat made me think that he'd dealt with death before. In my experience, collaborators don't usually have such strong stomachs.'

'But if Philippe isn't—what I thought he was . . . then it must be someone else who's behind all the trouble we've been having here.'

He shook his head slowly.

'*Au contraire.* Unhappily, even a war hero isn't necessarily an angel. What I wanted to check on was what Philippe might have on his conscience that would make him so very eager to get me out of the picture. And it seems that since he was able to return to Paris his operations have been on the sharp side, to say the least. Exactly how sharp, we don't know. But the report I got seems to show that he could still be a double-dealer. So instead of being ruled out, he's still very much ruled in.'

'Then what can we do now?' she asked despondently.

Simon consulted his watch, and finished his drink. He stood up and stretched himself, cat-like.

'Personally, I'm going to do a little exploring before dinner,' he told her cheerfully, and made a quick exit before she could press him further.

Back in his room, he changed quickly into the trousers which had been expendably damaged on his arrival, changed also into a pair of light but sturdy sneakers, and slipped into his hip pocket the flashlight which was as indispensable a part of his travelling necessities as the ordinary man's razor.

He left the château by the front door, with a nonchalantly affable wave to the gendarme standing there, who by this time seemed to have graduated from bewilderment to boredom with his comings and goings and changes of vehicle and costume. He headed around the side and downhill to the outbuilding where the late Gaston Pichot had fallen into the Hecate crypt.

The labourers whom he had seen at the barn were lounging outside. They appeared to ignore him as he passed, but continued to talk heatedly among themselves in hoarse *patois*, pitched too low for him to distinguish any words. Whatever the argument was about, there was evidently a

221

clash of strongly held opinions.

It was almost dark inside the storehouse and the Saint switched on his flashlight and allowed the beam to roam along the tiers of barrels stacked against the walls before turning it down into the hole that Gaston's fall had made. The underground chamber was empty—the Professor had either finished for the day or was busy elsewhere. He was not expecting any trouble at that stage, and the sounds of movement behind him did not register as a threat until it was almost too late.

CHAPTER SIX

HOW SIMON QUOTED FRANCOIS VILLON AGAIN, AND THE TEMPLAR TREASURE CAME IN HANDY

It nearly proved a painful lapse. The attack was swift and unexpected. Two powerful arms closed around his chest, squeezing the air from his lungs and almost lifting him clear off the ground.

Simon Templar's response was equally rapid and far more effective. The bear hug is a crude hold and easily broken by anyone not inhibited by a devotion to fair play, and when attacked without warning from behind the Saint considered himself absolved from the code of gentlemanly conduct.

His left heel lashed back in three drum-beat mule-kicks played on his attacker's left shin. The man yelped with pain and involuntarily let him down, enough to enable the Saint to stamp his full weight on to the assailant's right instep and grind it in. The reflex yelp hiccuped into a most satisfactory scream of real agony, and as the encircling pressure on him slackened the Saint sent both elbows driving back into the other's ribs. The restraining arms burst outwards like broken springs and he took one step forward and turned. The workman's chin could not have been better posed to receive the full impact of the Saint's uppercut.

Simon did not wait to watch him fall but sidestepped to meet the comrade who should by then have been using his body as a static punch bag. The man came in with an axe handle, flailing in a wide swing that even the most amateur of self-defenders would have treated with contempt. The Saint ducked low to let it swipe over him, and sprang up again to reward the unbalanced wielder with a chop of the back of the neck that put him down like the proverbial poleaxed ox.

From beginning to end that phase of the exercise had lasted no more than twenty-five seconds.

The Saint eyed the two remaining members of the hospitality committee speculatively. He stood completely at ease, legs slightly apart, hands hanging loosely at waist height as they closed in from either side. It would have taken more than two men to unsettle him at any time, even had they been experienced fighters. He knew that odds of two to one sound more frightening than they actually are, for the advantage is frequently with the one: he only has to look out for himself, while the two have to be careful not to hamper each other.

These two had not taken part in the original attack and now looked less than eager to launch a second one. Only loyalty to their fallen colleagues drove them nearer, and they might have seemed almost relieved when Mimette's shrill cry brought all the action to a sudden halt.

'*Arrêtez!* Stop it!'

Mimette ran between the two men and the Saint. Her cheeks were flushed and her eyes blazed with anger as she faced the workmen.

'Dubois. Arnould. *Vous êtes fous?* What do you think you're doing?' she demanded harshly.

Her arrival drained the last of the fight from them as effectively as if the Saint had drawn a gun. They looked sheepishly at her without answering.

'They may only have been trying to teach me some steps in the harvest festival dance,' Simon hazarded.

He stepped aside so that Mimette could clearly see the other sleeping duo behind him. She stared at the crumpled bodies and her voice shook as she asked: 'They're not—?'

The Saint laughed.

'No, just taking a short rest... *Attendez vous deux!*'

His voice cracked like a whip with authority, and the two workmen who were still on their feet stopped their furtive attempt to back away to the door.

Mimette faced them coldly.

'*Pourquoi?*'

The one called Dubois pointed rancorously at the Saint.

'Because he killed Gaston.'

'Really? So you know more than the police, do you?' she said sarcastically.

'Everything has gone wrong since he came here,' said the other sullenly. 'The men are saying he has reanimated the curse of the Templars.'

'You mean you are saying it, Arnould,' Mimette retorted. 'That is just superstitious nonsense. And Monsieur Templar did not kill Gaston.'

'Did you think that up all by yourselves, or did someone give you lessons?' Simon inquired of the men. 'And who suggested dealing with me on your own?'

The two men looked warily at each other and

225

each understood something that was not spoken. Dubois indicated the big man who had tried to bear-hug the Saint and was now beginning to stir back to an awareness of the world.

'It was his idea,' Dubois stated flatly.

'Louis?' Mimette scoffed. 'He's an ox. He never had an idea in his life.'

'Let it ride, Mimette,' said the Saint. 'They're not going to tell us unless we beat it out of them and I don't have the time.'

Both fallen warriors were now starting to climb back to the vertical. They glared murderously at the Saint but made no move to restart the battle.

'Take your friends and get out,' Simon told the deflated quartet, and they hurried to obey.

He waited until they had left before turning to Mimette.

'And what brought you to the rescue?' he asked as he retrieved his flashlight from where it had fallen during the scuffle.

'I was looking for you. When you told me about the car and Philippe it made me forget that I'd remembered.'

'You're getting confusing.'

'*Pardon.* What I meant was that while you were away I realised where I'd seen that drawing on the parchment before. There's something like it on the stone in the hall.'

'Interesting.'

226

She pouted.

'You don't seem very excited. I thought you'd be pleased.'

The Saint grinned mischievously.

'Allow me to upstage you.'

He moved over to the hole in the floor, switching on the flashlight as he began to descend the steps. The generator had been turned off, and except for the beam of his torch centred on the statue the chamber was in total darkness. Mimette joined him and shuddered as she gazed at the hideous figure.

'This is my party piece,' he said grandly. 'Watch carefully.'

He stepped over to the statue and operated the hidden mechanism. Slowly the section of wall swung back.

'*Violà*! How about that?'

Mimette was fascinated. The Saint shone his torch through the opening to show the passage beyond.

'How did you find it?' she asked at last.

'Luck,' Simon admitted candidly. 'To be honest, I didn't pay much attention to it at first. After all, there must be quite a few other tunnels and cellars under the château. Then I remembered something Louis Norbert had said, and it all fitted into place.'

'What was that?'

'When he was telling me about the Templars a few days ago, he mentioned that "*Ingare*" was

227

an anagram of "Regina". It didn't seem to mean much to him either—then. Later, Gaston fell into this chamber, complete with statue of Hecate. Still no significance, until you know that she was supposed to be Queen of the Underworld and the "guardian of the crossroads".' He tied a graphic knot in the air with his empty hand. 'Then it all slots together. She is the Regina the Templars referred to, and she's at a crossroads, albeit a hidden one. The parchment showed the tower and some squiggly lines underneath. I kept thinking it was a river, but it was a tunnel.'

Her lively intelligence was impatient to overtake him.

'So this passage leads to the tower?'

'It seems likely. Remember I told you I saw a man leave the tower and talk to the two villains who set fire to the barn? Well, he never reappeared, and I thought he must have kept behind the wall and beat it back to the château. No need if there was a tunnel running from the tower.'

'But that was before this place was found,' she argued.

He nodded.

'Yes. Which means there's another way in and out. I heard voices in the chapel, but I found only Louis there. My guess is that this passage links up with a tunnel running from the tower to the chapel.'

'And Norbert knows about it? But why didn't he say anything?'

'He certainly knows about it, and a good deal more. I'm sure of that,' Simon replied. 'I don't believe our Professor is altogether the dotty academic he likes people to think he is.'

'But surely you don't believe he could have killed Gaston?'

'No, I don't think he did that. I figure him more as a schemer than a doer. But I'll bet he has a fair idea who done it.'

She put a reflective finger to her lower lip.

'So you came down here to trace out the passage.'

'That was the idea, and still is,' he said.

'We'll go together,' announced Mimette.

He shook his head.

'No. This is my little project,' he said firmly. 'We're dealing with a murderer, and just in case I bump into him I'd rather not have you to worry about.'

'But . . .'

'No buts. I'll feel a lot better if I know that someone somewhere safe knows where I've gone. Go back to the château and wait. If I haven't surfaced in an hour or so, start ringing the alarm bells. OK?'

'I suppose so,' she agreed reluctantly.

Simon bent over and kissed her lightly on the nose.

'*A très tôt,*' he said softly.

He shone the beam of his flashlight on the ladder as she climbed up. She stopped at the top.

'Good luck, Simon.'

'I might need it,' he called back cheerfully, and with a wave of his hand he strode into the darkness of the passage.

For the first several paces the floor was smooth and straight, but then it began to veer and turn until even with his sense of direction he had trouble keeping track of it. The tunnel was cut through the solid rock of the hill, and was so irregular that at one moment he could not touch the roof and at others had to bend low to avoid hitting his head.

Counting his steps, he estimated that he had travelled nearly one hundred metres when the passage merged with another. His sense of direction told him that the left-hand branch would lead towards the château, and he decided to explore that one first. The tunnel became wider and straighter, and the air was remarkably fresh, indicating that the passage had certainly not been hermetically sealed for hundreds of years.

Presently the way began to slope upwards and the floor became smoother, the rock eventually giving way to flagstones.

He came to a couple of smaller passages that ran off on either side, but they dead-ended in a few yards, and he reckoned that he was now on the other side of some of the brick walls he had seen in the wine cellar.

Finally he found himself confronted by a heavy oak door. Like the one leading from the great hall to the chapel, it was studded with square-topped iron nails and had a heavy ring for a handle. He reached out, turned it—and pulled. The door opened soundlessly on recently oiled hinges.

He stood against the wall and waited, but there was no sound from the other side. After a moment, he opened the door wide and entered the room beyond.

It was long and rectangular, with a low slightly curved ceiling supported by four stout columns running down the centre. In alcoves along the walls rested coffins of stone or lead with the name of the knight they contained inscribed on the side. They were simple boxes, the complete opposite of the large, elaborately carved tomb that stood squarely in the centre of the crypt between the middle two columns. Its sides were adorned with what appeared to be battle scenes, and on top lay the figure of a Crusader, his armour covered by the overmantle of the Templars. His arms were folded across his chest, and his hands clasped the hilt of a huge double-edged sword that was almost as long as himself.

Hanging from each of the columns was a heavy battery lamp similar to those in the chamber the Saint had just left. Two were positioned so as to shed their light directly on to the tomb, while the others were angled to illuminate each end of the crypt.

He located the main connection and turned them on. In their cold light the crypt looked less sinister than it had by the shifting beam of his torch, but no more comforting. He could see the far end of the room for the first time. Starting from the centre of the wall was a flight of steps leading to a narrow landing which he figured would originally have been the entrance from the chapel.

The sarcophagus had clearly been designed to be the focal point of the room. At its foot was a small table of black marble that reminded him of some altars he had seen in side chapels in cathedrals, a smooth slab supported by four spiral columns rising from the floor. In the centre of the slab was a large oblong casket with a rounded lid.

As Simon bent to examine it, the door behind him slammed. He spun around and sprinted across the room, but knew even as he did so that it was a futile gesture. He hurled his weight at it, but he might just as well have battered himself against the stone wall it was set in. Nothing short of dynamite was going to make an impression on those four inches of seasoned oak.

The lock was massive, but given even the most rudimentary implement it would have been about as difficult to crack as a can of sardines. As far as the Saint was concerned, not having on him any such utensil, it might just as well have been the front door of Fort Knox.

He turned and walked the length of the room and mounted the steps at the end. It required no searching to locate where the door to the chapel had once been. Judging by the shape and size of the arch, it had probably been a twin of the one he had just been inspecting. Most of the entrance had been filled in with chunks of broken flagstones crudely mortared together and the gaps between them crammed with small stones. On the other side, he surmised, a much neater job must have been done, hiding the old opening completely, for he had noticed no sign of a doorway in the chapel other than the entrance from the great hall.

It was obvious that the way had been stopped for many centuries, probably when the château had replaced the fortress.

'But the Professor was tapping around the chapel looking for it,' he mused. 'And the second voice I thought I heard... somebody could have had a way out, like the man who came out of the tower and gave a package—of money?—to the arsonists... Therefore—'

He looked up. Directly above his head, a

rectangular opening had been cut in the ceiling. By the beam of his flashlight he could see through the thickness of the lath and plaster roof to the underside of flagstones. The stones in the centre of the hole seemed to be supported only by two beams of new wood.

By standing on his toes he could just touch the stone with his fingertips but it was impossible to exert enough pressure to lift it. He cast around the crypt for something to stand on, and saw again the casket at the foot of the master tomb.

Being imprisoned in a vault by a murderer and separated from the remains of devil-worshipping knights by a few centimetres of stone or lead is not a hilarious situation, but the smile that played on Simon Templar's lips was as genuine as any that ever lingered there. Running around in circles had never been his favourite method of keeping fit but had been the commonest form of exercise since his arrival at Ingare. The one incontrovertible, self-evident, and very definite result of his present discovery was that, for the moment at least, the running was over.

He felt a new vitality that came from the prospect of action. In less than an hour Mimette would raise the household and start a search, but instinct told him that by then there would be no need. His imprisonment, he was sure, was only meant to be temporary. Whoever was responsible would return to make quite certain he did not escape, and would come prepared. But not, perhaps, for the reception that the Saint might contrive to arrange.

He allowed himself a few moments to examine the casket. It was more than two feet long and almost a foot high. The metal was almost black, but a section of the lid and front had been cleaned to reveal the pure gleam of silver. In spite of the overall tarnish, it was possible to make out every detail of the embossed figures of knights and horses that formed a frieze around the edge of the lid. It had once been locked by a flap attached to the lid that fitted over a stanchion set halfway down the front and presumably secured by some form of padlock. Now both flap and stanchion were twisted and the lip of the casket was dented.

For such a rich container the contents seemed disappointingly dull. Inside was only a roll of parchment, brown with age and brittle to the touch. Carefully the Saint lifted it out and untied the two leather thongs at each end. He laid it beside the casket and delicately unrolled it until the first three or four inches became visible.

The parchment was so cracked and dark and the letters so faint that he had to strain his eyes to distinguish them. They ran in closely spaced lines without a break or capital to show where one word ended and another began. The last time he had seen such a text it had been in the clear print of a Bible appendix illustrating some of the original source material, with a translation underneath. For the first time since those days he wished he had paid more attention to the schoolmaster who had tried to convince him of the beauty of ancient Greek. Here and there he recognised a word or a short phrase, but not enough to make any sense of the meaning.

Even while he studied the scroll he was listening, alert now for the slightest sound. When he heard it, it was only a faint scrape of stone against stone. It came from the direction of the hole in the ceiling, and told him that someone was opening the improvised trapdoor in the chapel.

The Saint moved like lightning. He killed the lamps and padded as swiftly and silently as a ghost across the room. He was already standing against the wall beside the steps when the noise grew louder and a shaft of weak light speared the floor beneath the opening as the flagstone above was removed. He watched as a short ladder was lowered and a pair of legs climbed down.

They brought after them the dwarfish body and gnomish head of Professor Louis Norbert.

The professor stood for a moment regaining his breath, and switched on a flashlight. He directed the beam on to the floor and followed its path towards the plinth. The Saint fell soundlessly into step behind him. As they neared the centre of the crypt, Norbert raised the beam and stopped so abruptly when he saw the open casket that the Saint almost bumped into him.

Judging his moment with the timing of an actor, Simon tapped him on the shoulder.

'*Priez Dieu que tous nous veuille absouldre*,' he said sepulchrally.

It is physically impossible to jump out of one's skin, but Louis Norbert made the best attempt that the Saint had ever seen. His whole body jerked so violently that the flashlight flew from his hand. He whirled around but the Saint was no longer there. Simon side-stepped, picked up the torch and shone it straight into the professor's ashen face.

'*Bon soir, Maître.* How nice of you to drop in.'

'Templar!' Norbert gasped the name.

'Who were you expecting? Turn around slowly and raise your hands.'

'Why?' Norbert sounded genuinely puzzled.

'Because I'm getting cautious in my old age,' the Saint explained patiently, but with an edge to his voice that told the professor it would be wise to obey.

Norbert did as he was told and the Saint ran an expert hand over him.

'Excuse my suspicions, but one can't be too careful,' he remarked when he was satisfied that the most dangerous weapon the professor possessed was a fountain pen. 'Now let's have

237

more light on the subject.'

He moved across and switched on the lamps. He leant against one of the columns and eyed the professor thoughtfully. Norbert was staring at the casket.

'You have been reading the scroll?' he asked.

'I was trying to, but it's all Greek to me.'

Norbert appeared too relieved to enjoy the joke and was in a hurry to change the subject.

'How did you get in here?'

Simon indicated the locked door.

'Through there. Hecate let me in, and I just followed my nose.'

'You found the tunnel yourself?'

'Purely by luck—but whether it was good or bad remains to be seen,' replied the Saint. He pointed towards the parchment. 'What do you know about that piece of antique toilet paper?'

Norbert hesitated as he sought the right reply.

'Nothing much. Why should I?'

It was such an obvious lie that the Saint felt like laughing.

'Couldn't you understand it?'

Norbert shook his head, and even managed a half-hearted shrug.

'It is too fragile to unroll, without special treatment. And unhappily I am not very versed in ancient Greek. But from the few lines I have seen, it would appear to be a history of Ingare. Interesting in its own way, but no, not important.'

The Saint picked up the parchment. His eyes narrowed.

'A history of Ingare in ancient Greek,' he repeated. 'Obviously, not very interesting. So we needn't bother with it.'

With deliberate slowness he broke off a small corner and let it fall to the floor.

Norbert watched horrified as he prepared to repeat the operation. Suddenly he threw himself forward, clawing for the scroll, but the Saint was waiting for just such a move. He raised the parchment out of Norbert's reach as he pushed the little man away with the palm of his free hand.

'Well?'

Norbert glared at him in an impotent frenzy.

'I told you, it . . .'

'Try again.'

The professor looked from the scroll to the Saint and realised that the time for bluff was past. He spoke slowly and distinctly.

'It is the treasure of the Templars.'

Simon laid the parchment back on the marble slab beside the casket, his expression a mixture of perplexity and disbelief.

'This?'

Tenderly Norbert rolled it up, re-tied the thongs, and put it back in the casket and closed the lid. He turned to face the Saint.

'Yes, that is the treasure. No gold or jewels,

but something more priceless than any amount of them,' he announced calmly.

'But what is it?' Simon persisted impatiently.

'I believe...' the professor began and then stopped abruptly. He looked directly at the Saint, and his voice was almost defiant, as if he anticipated the response his words would receive. 'No, I am sure. It is the Testament of Judas Iscariot.'

The idea seemed so absurd that the Saint could hardly keep a straight face.

'The Gospel according to Judas? You'll have to do better than that.'

Norbert spread his hands in a gesture of resignation.

'I did not believe it either at first, but I have studied it as best I can. The writing, the parchment, everything can be scientifically dated and verified.'

'But surely Judas gave back the blood money and hanged himself. He didn't have time to write anything,' Simon protested.

Norbert's lips curled in a patronising smile.

'You were there? St Matthew says he hanged himself. In the Acts of the Apostles, it is written that after using the money to buy a field, later given the cursed name of Aceldama, he fell down and "burst asunder". Who knows? When the gospels were written—and remember, that was more than thirty years after the Crucifixion—it would be important to show that the man responsible for Christ's death had come to a bad end. How could the converts believe in a God that allowed such a man to live? It would have been an impossible question for them to answer.'

The professor was no longer looking at the Saint but at the casket. His hands were clasped at his waist and the original excitement in his voice as he revealed his discovery had given way to the dry monotone of a don addressing his students on an academic puzzle.

'There is no reason why he should not have escaped the wrath of the other disciples and later told his story to someone who wrote it down. Judas has always been an enigma, yet in many ways he is the second most important person in the gospels. Without Judas there might have been no Crucifixion, without a Crucifixion no Resurrection, and without a Resurrection no Christian religion. In his own way, he has a greater claim to sanctity than any of the other disciples.'

Simon was fascinated by the idea. 'St. Judas and All Traitors? That sounds like a fun parish. How did you find it—from the map or the stone?'

Norbert visibly stiffened.

'So you know about the map too,' he said slowly. 'Well, I suppose it does not matter now... No, not from the map or from the stone, but from my own observations. I, Louis

Norbert, discovered it. I did it all on my own. While he was chasing gold, I pursued truth. I solved the riddle the Templars left behind them. They were clever—clever enough to keep their secret for six hundred years, but not clever enough to fool me.'

The professor's voice had tightened until it almost choked him. His hands clenched and unclenched spasmodically as he spoke, and his staring eyes seemed to look straight through the Saint. For the first time Simon felt the real force of an obsession.

'The stone and the map were deliberately left to mislead. Why do you think they left them where they might be found? They were useless. Anyone who found them would search for a hoard of loot but find nothing, while the real prize was under their noses all the time. In there?'

Norbert pointed to the sarcophagus and then stepped towards it. His shaking hands caressed the recumbent figure sculpted on it.

'It was mere accident that neither the map nor the stone were found when the Templars left; but those who followed knew all about the tomb—and they ignored it, just a tomb in a crypt. Then they blocked up the crypt and even forgot about that. It was left to me, *me*, to open the crypt again and ask the questions no one else had asked. Why was it not in the chapel where all could see it? An important person's tomb,

242

but whose? There is no name on it. And why an altar at the foot of a tomb? To put something on. But what?'

Norbert grasped the corner of the sarcophagus beside the Crusader's left foot and pushed hard. The whole top slid halfway back on invisible rollers to reveal the hollow interior of the base, big enough to have held a giant's coffin, but now empty.

The professor chuckled.

'So simple, but so effective. And so safe. The Templars brought back many trophies from the Crusades, but this scroll was unique, and they kept it a secret. It was their treasure. They were accused of Devil worship. In the main it was a libel, but here at Ingare a cult must have developed around this unholy relic. And what greater prize for a Satanist than the words of the man who betrayed God?'

The Saint heard Norbert's words and their meaning registered, but he was no longer consciously listening to the little man's lecture. For a moment he was hardly aware of the present at all as his mind flooded with the images of the past.

He thought of the knights whose name he carried going out to do battle, their ideals as bright as their armour, their standards billowing in the wind of the charge. Fighting and dying and winning respect and renown. But when the campaigns were over, when there were no more pilgrims to protect or battles to win or walls to storm, growing rich and complacent and eventually corrupt. Accepting a life of luxury and indulgence, playing politics, storing wealth, and then at last dabbling in strange heresies against the faith that had first inspired them.

Instantaneously he remembered his own beginnings—the ideals that had sent him and his own small band of crusaders out into a world grown stale and lifeless from what was called progress. Ideals they had fought for and one had died for. To deliver justice in a world that no longer understood the word. To wage their own private war against the men who grew bloated on the lifeblood of the weak. Could it happen to him—a twentieth-century privateer akin to every soldier of fortune who had ever nailed his colours to the mast and set out to seek his destiny?

But that depressing prospect survived only a micro-second against the utterly gorgeous grandeur of the historic reality that had just exploded before his comprehension: a Templar treasure that could be truly priceless—and in ordinary terms completely unsaleable.

For a moment as his gaze swept over the lines of coffins he could wonder if one day he too would settle for a fading glory and the pleasures of the idle and the unconcerned. But only for that moment; and then he laughed. A deep, rich 'to hell with it all' laugh. The sword was still bright, and ideal was still a spur, and the jest was magnificent. So there was no treasure, just the words of a traitor. Something for the academics and theologians to argue over while the rest of the world carried on—business as usual. And a Nobel Prize or something of that sort for somebody, perhaps Louis Norbert.

'Of course, Henri knows about this,' said the Saint.

'He refuses to believe it,' Norbert said. 'He is still convinced of a treasure that can be counted or weighed and banked—'

At that same instant the key grated in the lock of the tunnel door. Before the startled professor realised what was happening he was engulfed in a whirlwind of action. The Saint killed the lamps, clamped a silencing hand over Norbert's mouth, and in a continuation of the same hold threw them both down behind the tomb.

The door swung open and the beam of a powerful flashlight carved the darkness. The Saint peered cautiously around the farthest side of the tomb. Standing in the splash of light just inside the doorway was Mimette, and from the awkward way she stood with her hands behind her he could tell without seeing them that they must be tied together there. At her side, a gun pressing into her ribs, was Henri Pichot.

3

There were fifteen feet of darkness between the

sarcophagus and the probing light source of Henri's torch. Had the Saint been alone, he would have asked for nothing more and cheerfully pitted his speed and stealth against the quickness of the lawyer's reactions. But even to attempt such a tactic now would have placed the girl in unacceptable danger, besides leaving Norbert free on his flank. Shielded by Mimette, within a pace of the open door and controlling the only light in the room, Henri's position was impregnable.

Stalemate. Henri, with no way of knowing whether the Saint was armed, could not approach further without putting himself at risk. The Saint, restricted by his hold on the professor, could not make any move that would take Henri by surprise. There was only one way the impasse could be broken, and Simon waited calmly for the inevitable, only slightly reassured by the conviction that his nerves were the stronger, and therefore every second that limped past, every fractional increase in the tension, must be to his advantage.

Henri swept the beam of his torch wildly around the crypt; but, hidden by the tomb on one side and the thickness of a column on the other, Simon stayed safely hidden. Only when the light told him that the beam was pointed another way would he steal a quick peep around the sarcophagus to keep track of captor and captive.

He weighed with icy detachment the significance of what he saw. Pichot's drawn features glimpsed in the dim illumination reflected by his flashlight from the walls, his too rigid stance offset by a slight trembling of the hand that gripped the automatic, revealed his inner desperation, and the Saint had found that there are few men more dangerous than a frightened amateur. By contrast, Mimette appeared almost relaxed. She stared straight ahead, her face calm and composed but her eyes wide and frozen. Grimly he recognised that shock would shield her for a short while, but if hysteria took over it would be a dangerous complication.

Still he waited.

Norbert began to wriggle, and the Saint was forced to shift his position slightly to straddle the professor's body, pinning his arms and legs against the floor. It made only the thinnest scuff of cloth against stone, but it was enough. The light beam swung towards the tomb, and when Pichot spoke his voice faltered and he could not quite control a rising pitch.

'Templar. I am going to count to three. Come out into the light with your hands up or I shall shoot Mimette.'

He spotlighted the floor a dozen feet away and jabbed the muzzle of his gun into the girl's side.

'One.'

Simon rolled off the professor and glided

towards the other end of the tomb. Behind him he heard Norbert clambering to his feet. Henri started and swung his flashlight towards the noise.

'No, don't shoot, it's me!' Norbert shouted frantically, and superfluously, as the light pinned him.

For a second, Pichot lost his place in the countdown.

'What are you doing here?' he rasped.

'I just came to have another look—'

'*N'importe*,' Henri cut him off. 'Templar, this is *two*!'

Perhaps the professor's appearance broke the spell or the first shock simply subsided, but at that moment Mimette snapped back into full personality.

'Simon?' she cried. 'Simon—if you are there, don't listen! This no-good—'

She began to strain furiously against the cord that bound her wrists. Henri grabbed her roughly around the waist and held her body against his own. His lips began to shape '*Three*'.

The Saint stepped out into the light.

He stood completely relaxed and regarded Henri Pichot with the ghost of a mocking smile pulling at the corners of his mouth.

'You've been watching too many old B movies, Henri. One, two, three, fire? How very unoriginal!'

Pichot ignored the taunt. The sight of the

Saint apparently surrendering injected a new confidence into his voice and actions. He called to the professor to turn on the lamps, and when the crypt was fully lit he shoved the girl towards the Saint, at the same time side-stepping so that he could keep them both covered.

'So the great Simon Templar isn't so clever after all,' he sneered, but the Saint only shook his head reproachfully.

'I'm sorry, Henri, but that isn't a unique observation either. You must get another writer. It's the stock line at the end of act three, scene two. I've seen the play more times than you.'

He put his arm around Mimette and drew her close. His main hope now was to play on Pichot's nerves until he goaded the lawyer into a mistake, while at the same time building up the girl's confidence until he could rely on her reactions. As a plan of campaign it was about as watertight as the *Titanic* but there was no alternative.

Henri gestured towards the tomb.

'Get over there.'

Still holding Mimette, Simon backtracked towards the foot of the sarcophagus until he felt the cold stone behind him. Norbert was standing on the other side of the tomb, his eyes switching uncertainly from Henri to the Saint. Pichot spoke without looking at him.

'Search him.'

The professor opened his mouth to speak,

hesitated, and in the end said nothing. He scuttled around the casket table and patted the Saint's clothes in the same way he himself had been checked over a short while before. His clumsiness made it impossible for Pichot to keep a steady bead on the Saint, and it would have been ridiculously easy to grab the little man and use him as a shield if it would not have meant leaving Mimette unprotected. Regretfully Simon let the opportunity pass.

Norbert turned to shake his head at Henri and the young lawyer smiled.

'No weapon? How reckless of you,' he observed, with a little more assurance.

Silently the Saint agreed, although he was inclined to place the oversight in the category of criminal negligence rather than mere recklessness. Aloud he said: 'I didn't know it was going to be this kind of party. Anyway, I thought pokers were more in your line.'

He was surprised by the effect his words had on Norbert. As soon as Henri had entered the crypt, Simon had accepted the lawyer's guilt as a matter of fact and had since been mentally fitting the pieces of the pattern into place. He knew that Mimette must already have observed the revelation, and in the same way he had assumed the professor to be Henri's full partner and had not given that association a second thought. Now he realised that his assumption had been wrong.

'Henri! No! *You* killed Gaston?'

There was no doubting the genuineness of Norbert's shocked disbelief.

Henri's lips curled. He was clearly beginning to enjoy his moment in the centre of the stage.

'Why so astonished, Professor?' His tone was bitingly sarcastic. 'Scruples? They never bothered you before.'

'But not murder!' Norbert protested vehemently. 'You told me—'

'What I thought you would accept. To keep you quiet, while I could use you.'

'But why kill Gaston, Henri?' demanded Mimette fiercely. 'What did your uncle ever do to hurt you?'

Simon supplied the answer, working out the details as he spoke them.

'He realised that Henri was trying to ruin the business, but he hesitated to expose his own nephew. He tried to warn me by telling me not to trust anyone, whoever they might be, but I was still thinking about Philippe. I should have realised that Henri was the only one who could have stirred up the workers against me. He was the only one they would have listened to, they were his friends and he'd grown up among them.'

Pichot said tonelessly: 'He kept going on about loyalty, about the family. Like all the Pichots he was a serf at heart. He couldn't understand that the Florians are not royalty and

251

Ingare is not a kingdom. Only I had the will and the brains to outgrow that antiquated mental bondage. He wouldn't see that we had as much right to the treasure as the Florians, if we found it. He told me he was going to show the map to Yves. I couldn't let that happen.'

The Saint had always been mildly sceptical about the propensity of storybook villains for unravelling their own mysteries in the final showdown scene, but if Henri was determined to conform to that convenient convention he was not going to discourage him.

'After all,' he prompted, 'you'd gone to a lot of trouble to get it.'

'For years I've searched for it,' said Pichot forcefully. 'Why do you think I kept coming back here, Mimette? So you and your father could patronise me?'

'We should have known better than to expect any gratitude for all we'd done for you,' she retorted scornfully.

Norbert sagged against the side of the tomb. His face was grey and he clutched at the stone to steady himself. The self-satisfaction of a few minutes before was gone as if it had never existed.

'But you said there would be no violence. You promised!' he protested furiously. 'Just let Philippe get control of the château, and he would put you in charge and we could look for the treasure openly . . .'

Pichot's clipped humourless laugh cut through the professor's spluttering.

'And you believed me. You're a fool, Professor. You even thought the séance was for real. Philippe's interest in buying Ingare was waning. I had to use the treasure as a bait to make him stay. A message from the dead. It was a good idea, but Templar spoiled it, just as he threatened to spoil everything.'

'So when you went prepared to kill Gaston, you also went prepared to frame me for it,' said the Saint. 'And when even that didn't work, you tried to kill Yves by jiggering the brakes on his Mercedes. Which didn't kill either of us. Not having a great deal of success, are you, Henri?' he concluded with mocking sympathy.

'Success?' Pichot seemed to savour the word. 'Perhaps not at first, but it could not have worked out better. I heard you and Mimette talking about exploring the tunnel, and then I saw how I could still get Ingare and dispose of you both as well.'

The nervous tension that he had shown when he pushed Mimette into the crypt was only a shadow behind his eyes. He was confident now of his control of the situation and relishing the power it gave him.

'Do tell us how,' Simon invited.

'You and Mimette will simply disappear. Have you eloped together? No—you have kidnapped her. In a few days the ransom notes

253

begin to arrive. One from Marseille, I think—
yes—and the next from Paris. A piece of
Mimette's jewellery with each one. And then,
nothing.'

'Except my car left here.'

'Abandoned because it was too conspicuous.
When you went to Carpentras, you arranged to
be picked up by an accomplice.'

'Very neat.'

'Without his precious daughter, Yves will not
have the heart to hold out for long against
Philippe, and I will be free to find the treasure.
So you see I do win in the end.'

'But I have found the treasure,' Norbert
insisted. 'I told you.'

Pichot snorted derisively. He pointed with his
free hand to the casket, but his gun never
wavered from its aim at the Saint's chest.

'That scroll? You must think me as naïf as
you are, Professor. But the box, that is valuable,
and there will be more like it, with more
precious things in them.'

'But the map was a trick, don't you
understand?' pleaded Norbert passionately.

Pichot's pudgy face set into harder lines, and
there was a more dangerous coldness in his eyes.

'It is you who are trying to trick me. You
want the treasure for yourself. Be careful,
Professor, or perhaps the Saint will shoot you as
he kidnaps Mimette.'

For a moment he appeared to be thinking out

that possibility, and then slowly he nodded.

'Yes, it might be better that way in any case. I don't need you any more. I can't trust you. We shall see. Open the tomb, Professor. It will be a fitting resting place for a Florian and a Templar.'

'I would prefer it to the company of at least one Pichot,' said Mimette disdainfully.

Simon Templar knew that he had to make his final assessment of the situation, but from whichever angle he considered it the scales were always tipped in the lawyer's favour. He and Mimette were standing near the altar, while Norbert was towards the other end of the tomb, a few feet from Henri. The way Henri gripped his automatic told the Saint that he was not accustomed to handling firearms, but with only a dozen feet between them he could hardly miss even a moving target. To attempt to tackle him without any diversion would merely hasten the end for both himself and Mimette.

Simon put his left arm across Mimette and pressed her back so that his body partly shielded her. He moved smoothly, easily, intent on making his action look like a chivalrous gesture rather than a threat, but combining it with a step of his own that brought him half a pace closer to the casket.

'Stay where you are,' rasped Henri. 'Professor, I said open the tomb.'

Pichot raised his gun, and his finger looked

tight on the trigger. The Saint braced himself for the spring that he had to make even though he knew it would almost certainly be useless. And at that instant something seemed to snap inside the professor.

'No!' he shouted, and launched himself towards Pichot like an infuriated elf.

Henri had been concentrating on the Saint and Mimette and had to turn sideways to meet the unexpected attack. Norbert was blundering and clumsy, but his hands were already clawing at the gun when Henri fired.

Norbert screamed and fell, still clinging to the sleeve of Henri's coat, but the lawyer kicked viciously at his chest as he went down and the hold was broken. Henri swung around to face the Saint again, but the Saint was no longer there.

He did not try to reach Henri. Even with the advantage of the distraction Norbert had caused, he could not have covered the ground fast enough. But the casket he could reach in one stride. Pushing Mimette away, he leapt towards the altar as Henri turned.

He picked up the heavy casket with both hands and in the same continuous flowing movement sent it hurtling through the air.

Pichot fired, but it was a wild reflex action, and the bullet scraped the top of the tomb and ricocheted harmlessly away. He had no time for another shot. The casket smashed into the side of his head and he went down without a sound. The automatic spun from his hand, and the Saint dived for it and caught it before it reached the floor.

Simon rolled over and up to his feet, but when he saw Henri's face he knew he would not need the gun.

4

The edge of the casket had opened a gash from Henri's cheekbone to his chin as it smashed into the side of his face and most probably broke his jaw. He lay on his back, his arms flung out, and only the rasp of irregular breathing showed that he remained to be counted among the living.

Simon retrieved and pocketed the automatic as he stepped over him, and knelt beside the professor. Norbert was moaning faintly, lying on his side and clutching at the top of his leg. Unceremonious pulling down of his trousers revealed that the slug had passed through the fleshy inside of his thigh but managed to miss both bone and artery. It was a fairly tidy wound and not dangerous provided the bleeding was stopped soon.

Mimette came over, and the Saint stood up and greeted her with a grim smile.

'He'll live. They both will,' he said tersely as he untied her hands.

She gazed down at Henri and shuddered.

'I've known him all my life. I still can hardly

257

believe he did such things. The family was always so good to him.'

'Perhaps that was the trouble. To some people, kindness is an unforgivable insult,' Simon remarked cynically. 'I'll see to these two while you go and summon our amiable gendarme and call an ambulance.'

Mimette nodded and turned towards the tunnel, but he stopped her and pointed to the ladder.

'You'd better use the professor's private entrance. It'll be shorter.'

She saw the trapdoor for the first time and her brow furrowed, but the Saint forestalled her questions.

'You'll understand as soon as you get out. Just do it quickly.'

She hurried towards the far end of the room and Simon turned back to Norbert. He commandeered the professor's large handkerchief and tore it into three equal strips which he knotted together, and bound the improvised bandage around Norbert's leg, to hold pads of cloth ripped from the professor's shirt-tails in place over the bullet's entrance and larger exit hole, which staunched the worse of the bleeding.

The old man was returning to full awareness as the shock that had helped mask the pain was wearing off. He whimpered as the necessary pressure was applied to the dressing, and his face was pale and drawn as he looked up at the Saint.

'I'm sorry,' he began weakly. 'I didn't understand. I was a fool. I . . .'

Simon cut him short.

'Save it. It isn't me you're going to have to make your excuses to. As far as I'm concerned, we can call it quits. If you hadn't gone for Henri when you did, I probably couldn't have taken him.'

He took another look at the lawyer. Pichot was still unconscious and was likely to remain so for some time. The Saint had no idea how efficient the local ambulance service might be, but given the château's isolation there was likely to be a considerable delay before they arrived. If the professor was going to get the prompt treatment he needed, a car might be a faster solution.

'This may hurt,' Simon warned, and before Norbert fully understood his meaning he found himself slung in a fireman's lift across the Saint's shoulders. He yelped at the sudden pain and all but fainted as he was carried to the ladder.

The opening was only a couple of feet wide, and the Saint had to shift his burden and carry it piggyback fashion until his head and shoulders were through the opening. As gently as possible he rolled Norbert on to the altar carpet that had previously concealed the trapdoor, and was

259

climbing the last few rungs when the door from the great hall opened.

Led by Sergeant Olivet and followed by three gendarmes, Mimette, Philippe, and Yves rushed down the chapel towards him.

'That was quick,' Simon remarked as they reached him. 'How did you get here—by one of Hitler's left-over V2s?'

Olivet returned his smile.

'I was already here. Monsieur Florian called me.'

The Saint looked questioningly at Yves, who shook his head.

'He means Philippe.'

'Well, well, well,' Simon drawled. 'Today is full of surprises.'

He watched Philippe thoughtfully while Olivet was directing the transport of Norbert to hospital. The industrialist was subdued and without a trace of the arrogance that had grated on the Saint ever since his arrival at Ingare. By contrast Yves looked tired but no longer defeated, and there was a new strength to the fingers that grasped Simon's hand. Mimette had a look in her eyes that told him her private thanks would be worth waiting for.

'I don't know how we are ever going to repay you,' said Yves fervently.

'Right now I'll settle for a drink,' Simon replied lightly.

He turned to Olivet, as the sergeant finished

giving instructions to the two men who now had the professor seated in a chair formed by their interlocked arms. As they carried him from the chapel a vague sound of movement drifted up from the crypt.

'Your murderer awaits,' said the Saint with a flourish of his hand towards the opening in the floor. 'I'm afraid he's a bit damaged, but I've left his neck intact for your official chopper.'

'*Vous êtes trop gentil*,' Olivet said, with saturnine gravity.

He drew his pistol and climbed down the ladder. Simon waited until the remaining gendarme had followed his leader into the crypt before suggesting that the drink he had already mentioned was long overdue.

As they walked back through the great hall towards the centre of the château he told them about the scroll and his conversation with Norbert. Yves and Mimette speculated excitedly about the find but Philippe hardly seemed to hear. He trailed along behind them without speaking and avoided the eyes of anyone who glanced at him.

It was Philippe the Saint wanted to talk to, but it was more than two hours before he was allowed the chance, when Henri had been taken away and both he and Mimette had made their statements.

Finally the gendarmes left and he was able to ask the question that Olivet himself had not put.

261

He sank more comfortably into his chair and looked across the salon to where Philippe was opening a new bottle of Scotch.

'So you called the cops, Philippe?' he said quietly. 'And told them that Henri was a prime suspect. Why?'

Philippe seemed almost relieved that the question had been asked at last. He sighed deeply and his voice came low and stiffly apologetic.

'Because I knew one thing that you did not. I knew that I did not kill Gaston. Last night I thought—no, I hoped—that it was you who had done it. I didn't want to face the alternative.' Philippe paused and looked at his half-brother. 'You see, Yves, I knew that Henri was trying to ruin Ingare. Oh, I had no actual proof, but it was clear that only he could be behind all that had happened. I wondered sometimes if he thought he was doing me a favour. But of course he believed that if I got control I would put him in charge.'

'And you did nothing to stop him?' stormed Mimette, her eyes sparkling with anger and a deep flush colouring her cheeks. 'How could you?'

Philippe continued to address Yves, trying to meet his eyes.

'Believe me, I did not intend to let it go too far. You must believe that. I was only waiting for conclusive evidence that it was Henri. But in

262

the meantime, I hoped that what he was doing would force you to see sense. To see that the old ways are no longer good enough, that running a vineyard is a business, not a pastime. I wanted to make you move into the twentieth century...'

'By bankrupting us? How kind!' said Mimette scathingly, and Philippe turned on her with a show of his old aggression.

'No, by making you accept my kind of help. Then I could have insisted on doing what had to be done to make Ingare viable again.'

The Saint intervened quickly to head off the confrontation.

'But that still doesn't explain why you thought Henri killed Gaston,' he said.

Philippe refilled his glass before replying. He held it close to his face and gazed into the light golden liquid.

'I knew the old man suspected his nephew. He had guessed, just as I had. The more I thought about it, the more I realised that Henri was the only one with a motive. Even then I couldn't believe that that would make him commit murder. But this afternoon I searched his room.'

He drew a small dog-eared notebook from his pocket and tossed it on to the coffee table in the centre of the room.

'I found that. The writing inside is Gaston's. Something about treasure and a tunnel. There is an old parchment map too. They had to be what the murderer was looking for when he ransacked the cottage. So I called Olivet. Perhaps fortunately, Henri had convicted himself before I had to produce this evidence. So you can keep it in the most secret archives of Ingare.'

There was an extended silence, while each of those present digested the various implications of what had been revealed.

After some time, Yves voiced what might have been a general question: 'I wonder what Henri and Louis will say when they are interrogated.'

'They can only involve each other,' said the Saint confidently. 'They were both using each other, with different motives. Henri is much smarter, in a lawyer's way—he was clever enough to defend me, when Philippe was accusing, which made it look as if he had no need of a scapegoat—but Norbert is such an obviously genuine archaeological nut that he's pretty sure to get off on the grounds of idiocy. Also in consideration of having finally tried to stop Henri putting down two more victims.'

Mimette shivered.

'Simon was magnificent,' she said. 'But for him—'

'I was temporarily deranged,' Simon contradicted her firmly. 'Or how could I have turned down the chance of sharing a coffin with

264

such a delightful companion?'

Yves Florian pressed his fingertips together, almost an attitude of prayer, with a half-smile on his lips but a deeper tautening of the muscles around it.

'Simon is now one of the family,' he said. 'I think that the private affairs of our family—including Philippe—can be trusted to his discretion.'

The Saint met his eyes in a long steady acknowledgement.

'*D'accord.*' With a deliberate lightening of the intensity, he scanned the room as if in search of a missing person. 'By the way, what happened to Henri's girl?'

Mimette pouted.

'Jeanne Corday? Charles told me she sent for a taxi and left in a hurry this afternoon. She must have decided that Henri was too much of a problem.'

'I expect she'll survive,' Simon said cheerfully. 'I'll have to look her up next time I'm in Paris.'

To dodge the invisible daggers that Mimette launched at him, he turned hastily to Yves.

'Well, if the parchment in that casket really is the testament of Judas Iscariot, your money troubles are over. You can either sell it to a museum for a fortune or keep it here and charge everybody admission to come and see it. The Ingare Scroll. And put on a full production of the Château's History in *son et lumière*'.

'I think I will keep it here where it has been for so long,' said Yves reflectively. 'But I have a better name for it. It shall be known as the Templar Scroll. What do you think of the idea, Simon?'

The Saint stretched his legs in front of him and sipped his drink as he considered the proposal.

'Yes,' he said at last. 'I rather like that.'

He thought of his namesakes in the crypt, and the thousands more who had fallen on the battlefields of the Crusades, and added quietly to himself: 'But would they?'

WATCH FOR THE
SIGN OF THE SAINT

HE WILL BE BACK

Photoset, printed and bound in Great Britain by
REDWOOD BURN LIMITED, Trowbridge, Wiltshire